AWARDS AND PRAISE FOR
QUID PRO QUO

Ann Connor Brimer Award nominee
Arthur Ellis Award for Best Juvenile Crime Novel
Bank Street College List of Best Books selection
CBC Radio's Young Canada Reads winner
Canadian Library Association Children's Book of the Year nominee
The Edgar Allan Poe Award nominee
New Jersey Library Association's Garden State Teen Book Award nominee
A New York Public Library Best Book for Teens selection
Red Cedar Award nominee
Silver Birch Award nominee

★ "The kind of timing, pacing, deadpan one-liners, and punchy humour
that a seasoned stand-up comic would envy…both real and funny."
—*Quill & Quire*, starred review

"A very, very funny book. I couldn't put it down."
—CBC Radio's Children's Book Panel

"The narrator of this thoroughly engaging whodunit is the smartest
mouth on two legs any of us could expect to meet." —*The Globe and Mail*

"Funny, clever! Four and a half stars." —*Today's Parent*

"Hilarious…A clever plot twist or two, a lot of laughs and a new favorite
narrator." —Knight Ridder News Agency

"Humor, wackiness, intelligence, and suspense—what else would we
wish for?" —*KLIATT* magazine

"A brilliant mystery-adventure novel." —*Canadian Children's Book News*

QUID PRO QUO

VICKI GRANT

ORCA BOOK PUBLISHERS

Library and Archives Canada Cataloguing in Publication

Grant, Vicki, author
Quid pro quo / Vicki Grant.

Originally published: Victoria, B.C.: Orca Book Publishers, ©2005.
Issued in print and electronic formats.
ISBN 978-1-4598-1931-3 (softcover).—ISBN 978-1-4598-1932-0 (PDF).—
ISBN 978-1-4598-1933-7 (EPUB)

I. Title.
PS8613.R367Q52 2018   jc813'.6   C2017-907919-0
C2017-907920-4

First published in the United States, 2018
Library of Congress Control Number: 2018933703

Summary: This humorous novel for middle readers is also a legal thriller that follows
Cyril MacIntyre as he uses every skill he has to find his missing mother.

*Orca Book Publishers is dedicated to preserving the environment and
has printed this book on Forest Stewardship Council® certified paper.*

Orca Book Publishers gratefully acknowledges the support for its publishing
programs provided by the following agencies: the Government of Canada through the
Canada Book Fund and the Canada Council for the Arts, and the Province of British
Columbia through the BC Arts Council and the Book Publishing Tax Credit.

Cover design by Teresa Bubela
Author photo by Megan Tansey Whitton

ORCA BOOK PUBLISHERS
orcabook.com

Printed and bound in Canada.

21 20 19 18 • 4 3 2 1

For my father—Robert B. Grant, DFC—
because he would have gotten a kick out of this.

And for my children—Augustus, Teddy and Roo—
because he would have gotten a kick out of them too.

Amor vincit omnia.
—V.G.

Quid pro quo (kwid pro kwo) **(Latin)**
"What for what"

A legal term meaning an even
exchange between two people

Something that is given
in exchange for something else

CONTENTS

CHAPTER ONE

Disclosure
The act of fully revealing the facts of a case

I started going to law school when I was ten years old.

I love saying that. I love how people look at me like, *this guy must be some kind of genius.*

It's true too.

Well, like, sort of true anyway.

I did start going when I was ten. But that's only because we didn't have any money for babysitters, so I got dragged to all my mother's night classes.

I hated it. You think math class is bad. Law school was unbelievably boring. I wasn't allowed to move or "make one single sound, so help me God, Cyril." I had to just sit there while the professors yakked on and on about torts and fiduciary rights and the "crumbling skull" doctrine, which sounds good but is just as boring as all the other legal garbage.

The only thing worse than class was helping my mother study for exams. She'd get so stressed out I'd have to read her the study questions over and over again. She actually made me pull a couple of all-nighters with her just to make sure she was prepared.

And then there were the term papers. She treated me like I was her own personal little library slave. I had to run around getting her the ten-pound books she needed, or photocopy six thousand pages of statutes while she two-finger-typed her essay or—get this—went outside for a smoke.

If I ever complained, she'd completely flip out. She'd start screaming how I was so ungrateful! How she was doing this for me! So I could have a better life—not her!

Blah, blah, blah.

I used to argue with her. If you ask me, a better life for a kid is playing *Zombie Komando* or hanging with his friends, not sitting in a smoky kitchen until three in the morning, helping his mother study for her civil-procedures exam. (Hadn't she ever heard what secondhand smoke does to children's delicate lungs?)

I wouldn't argue with her now though. I hated law school, but if I hadn't spent three years of my life there, I wouldn't have known anything about fraud, blackmail or the principle of equity.

In other words, I wouldn't have known what I needed to know to save my mother's life.

CHAPTER TWO

Fillius nullius (Latin)
"Son of nobody"—an illegitimate child

You need some background info.

My name is Cyril Floyd MacIntyre. I'm fourteen. My mother's legal name is Andrea Ruth MacIntyre, but everyone calls her Andy. She's twenty-nine.

You do the math.

Pretty nasty, eh?

She ran away from home and was living on the streets when she had me. That was enough to horrify her parents. Most teenagers would have been happy to leave it at that. But Andy really wanted to humiliate them, so she named her little fatherless love child Cyril, then threw in Floyd just to make them crazy. Those are poor-people names. Names for people who didn't go to school long enough to know that Thomas or Adam or Douglas would be more appropriate. Not names for a "good family" like the MacIntyres.

That's all I know about my grandparents. Maybe they were horrible. I don't know. But I think they had a point about the name.

I'm five foot one and, after a major feed, ninety-two pounds. If you can't picture what that looks like, here's a hint: pathetic.

Boney Maroney.

Mr. Puniverse.

Stick Man.

I've heard them all. I'm hopeful puberty will improve my stats, but I can't count on it. Andy seems to be about normal height for a woman, so that's not giving me any clues, and she either won't tell me or doesn't know who my father is. He might be some scrawny guy that she just felt sorry for one night, and this is as tall as I'm going to get. Or he could be some six-foot-three hunk that she fell for, and there's hope. I guess I'll know one way or the other in a couple of years.

I only know three things about my father. That he was white. That he was male. (Hey, I'm no fool. I aced sex ed.) And that he probably had brown eyes. I'm just guessing on the last one. Andy's got blue eyes, and I have brown. When we did genetics in science, the teacher said two blue-eyed people don't usually have a brown-eyed kid. She didn't say anything about hair. It wouldn't have helped anyway. I have this kind of fuzzy memory of Andy's hair being purple and spiked, but now it's…I don't know, brown, I guess. Reddy brown. Like mine. We have the same dimples, the same freckles and, apparently, the same hands. As far as I can figure out, I didn't get much from my father.

Not any money, that's for sure. Andy got us this far all by herself.

Okay, not 100 percent all by herself. Community Services kept us off the street, but she turned herself around. You got to give her credit for that. She doesn't do drugs anymore. She doesn't drink, unless you call a beer now and then drinking. And she hasn't shoplifted since the time she ran out of diapers a week before the next social-assistance check was due. (That wasn't Andy's fault though—at least, according to her. It was mine. Any other kid would have been toilet trained by then, and she never would have had to resort to stealing. Only two and a half, but already I was accessory to a crime.)

Andy does smoke like a chimney, swear like a sailor and eat a lot of crap. Nobody can believe that anyone who lives on burgers and extra-sauce donairs can stay that skinny. I figure she burns up a lot of calories being so pissed off all the time. As far as she's concerned, most people are imbeciles. (That's not the exact word she uses, of course. She usually goes for something a little more—ah, let's just say *colorful*.) She's always shooting her mouth off at somebody— and I'm always the one apologizing for it.

That's her bad side, and she knows it. She's trying to "deal with her anger" and has been for as long as I can remember. She's not a bad person though. She's actually a pretty good person, once you get past all the irritating stuff. She's generous, kind and forgiving—way more than most people who do the big "generous, kind and forgiving" thing. She'll call a person an imbecile one minute and give them the last of her French fries the next.

I love her.

I guess all kids love their mothers. Most kids just don't have as many reasons not to.

CHAPTER THREE

LLB

The abbreviation of the Latin term for the bachelor of laws degree

Law school was a drag, so I was really happy when Andy finally graduated.

I was sitting there watching that big fancy graduation ceremony, waiting for the M people to be called, and my heart was pounding like I was the one who was going to have to get up onstage.

I mean, I was so happy.

Not because there wouldn't be any more stupid exams. Not because there wouldn't be any more stupid tuition payments. Just because she did it. A high-school dropout with a big mouth and a kid to look after had made it through law school. There were guys from rich families and private schools who couldn't hack it—but Andy did. You've got to admit, that's something.

She was smiling her face off when her name got called, and (I'm not kidding) I thought I was going to cry when the dean of the law school handed her the diploma and gave her a hug. That was amazing. She'd driven him nuts for three years, always ranting on about something or other.

"There are too many white, male professors!"

"The cafeteria is anti-dog-owner!"

"The soap in the women's washroom is environmentally unfriendly...and the wrong color pink... and not soft enough on my delicate hands!"

Whatever.

Andy was always standing up for what's "right." Can you imagine anything more irritating? I'd just sink down in my chair and pretend it wasn't happening. I don't think the dean could do that. He had to read her petitions, meet with her protest groups—you know, act like he cared. So it was really nice that he hugged her at the graduation ceremony. It showed he knew that her heart was in the right place at least.

It was kind of sad at the party afterward though. Craig Benvie, this really straight guy in her legal ethics class, had the hots for Andy, so he hung around as usual. Jeannie Richardson was talking to her again, but not like she used to. Most of the older students, who had families too, were still nice to her, but everyone else had had enough of Andy by then. They shook her hand and said, "Good luck," but you knew they were really thinking, Good riddance.

Lots of guys from her class were going to Toronto or Vancouver or one of the fancy law firms down on the Halifax waterfront. Andy went on and on about how that grossed her out, about how she wouldn't stoop to work for "a bunch of corporate *imbeciles* whose only interest in the law is to see how much money they can squeeze out of their sleazy clients," but I didn't really believe her. I think she was pissed off she didn't even get a job interview with any of the big firms. She hates it when people think they're better than she is.

Me, I was just glad she got any job. Her marks were okay, but I bet she stank in the interviews. I know what she's like with "people in authority," especially people in authority she needs something from. She gets all snotty, like they're the ones asking for the favor.

I guess that didn't bother Atula Varma. She hired Andy as her articling student. That's sort of an apprentice. Everyone has to work in a law firm for, like, a year before they can become a real lawyer. You don't get paid very much to article—especially if you're articling for Atula.

I'm not saying it's Atula's fault. It's just the way things are. Those giant law firms make tons of money, so it's no big deal for them to pay their articling students a living wage. Atula had this one-woman law firm in this really cheesy part of town. Her clients were poor. They couldn't pay her much, so she couldn't pay Andy much. But who cared? It was a lot more than Andy was making babysitting the upstairs neighbor's kid.

Atula's kind of like Andy, actually. She's one of those people who say what they're thinking even if other people aren't going to like it, one of those people who seem a lot worse than they are. She doesn't smile much, but that doesn't mean she isn't nice.

She was always giving me clothes her son had grown out of. She even gave me this Hilfiger sweatshirt that I really liked until Andy made me cover the brand name with hockey tape because no kid of hers was going to be "a walking advertisement for some huge multinational corporation."

Typical Andy.

It's not okay to wear a brand-name sweatshirt, but it is okay to eat at McDonald's every night. Like McDonald's isn't a huge multinational. Andy just likes their fries better than the ones Camille Dubaie makes at his fish-and-chip shop downstairs.

Atula has this big social conscience too, but at least she's reasonable about it. She lets her kid have a cell phone. (Andy won't let either of us have one.

She's convinced the phone company's listening in on all our fascinating conversations about my homework and personal hygiene.) Atula does mostly immigration law—you know, helping new people get into the country—but she'll pretty much take on any legal problems her clients have.

And they've got a lot. You wouldn't believe how screwed up their lives are. These aren't the kind of people who are suing each other for big bucks because their real estate deal went bad. They're fighting with their ex-boyfriend over who gets to keep the waffle-maker.

Or they're fighting with their landlord over the stain on the hall carpet.

Or they're fighting with the government to get thirteen more dollars on their welfare check.

Or they're trying to get somebody to help them cover the cost of drugs for their kid with the kidney problem.

That wouldn't amount to a lot of money to most people, but it does to them. These guys have nothing.

I mean, nothing.

You're probably wondering how I know so much about Atula's clients.

Simple.

My mother's insane.

CHAPTER FOUR

Non compos mentis (Latin)
A legal term meaning "not of sound mind"

I mean it. Andy's insane.

Nuts. Wacko. Certifiable. I'm amazed nobody's locked her up yet.

Okay, well, they have. But that's different. I'll get to that later.

Anyway, last summer, I thought, was going to be the sweetest summer ever.

Now that we were "rich"—ha-ha—Andy wanted to get a babysitter for me, but I managed to convince her that twelve going on thirteen was too old to be babysat. And no matter what she said, I was not going to go to that stinking day camp again for, like, the tenth year in a row.

It wasn't easy, believe me. She's so paranoid. Normally the only thing she lets me do by myself is go to the bathroom, and even then she hovers around outside the door half the time. I don't know what's the matter with her. It's like she thinks if I'm out of her sight for one minute, I'm going to start smoking crack or get a girl pregnant (like *that* could ever happen).

Anyway, she must have been really happy about starting her new job, or maybe she just wanted to try something different and be reasonable for a change, but this time it worked. I whined and sulked and wouldn't play cribbage with her for about two weeks straight, and she finally caved. She gave me, like, 147 rules of appropriate behavior—but who cared? In the end, she actually agreed to let me look after myself for a while.

I had the two best weeks of my life, hanging out at the skateboard bowl with Kendall Rankin. It was great. I finally learned how to do an ollie, and my pop-shove-it was getting excellent. This one girl even said "wow" when I did it. Runts like me don't usually get that kind of reaction from girls like Mary MacIsaac.

Then Andy found out Kendall wasn't spending the summer with his father in Moncton like I'd sort of suggested he was, and that was the end of that. I didn't know what she had against Kendall. She'd decided he was a bad influence on me.

So what if all he wanted to do was skateboard? Like that was so criminal? At least he was good at it. At least he wasn't taking drugs and hanging out with losers, like she was at his age (unless, of course, she considers me a loser).

Don't even get me started talking about Kendall and Andy. All I'm saying is that for some crazy reason (i.e., she's crazy) I couldn't hang out at the bowl anymore. I had to go to Atula's and help out at the office.

Unpaid, of course.

So that's how—despite my best efforts to pretend they didn't exist—I got to know so much about Atula's clients.

I spent virtually all last summer in this unbelievably gross office. Just to give you some idea what it was like, the *Varma and Associates* sign was a piece of green bristol board taped to the door. Atula's printing was pretty neat, but still! A Magic-Markered sign?!? It doesn't really give the best first impression, especially when there's this note scrawled below it that says *Please keep your voices down! This is a law office!!!!* Like that would really make you feel like you're hiring top-notch legal counsel.

I guess, though, by the time you made it upstairs to see the sign you'd know not to expect any three-hundred-dollar-an-hour lawyer. For starters, all you could smell when you walked in off the street was—I don't know. Something gross. Like pee. Or a tuna sandwich left in a locker maybe. Or a dead rat. It was enough to make me gag. I always took a big breath before I opened the door and then just bolted up the stairs to the office.

Anyway, my job was to answer the phone. At least, that was my official job. What I was really doing was keeping the clients out of Atula's hair so she could get some work done. I sat in this little waiting room behind a big wooden desk that had a can of chicken-noodle soup holding up one leg. When the phone rang I was supposed to get all the details I could from the client. If it was urgent, I had to knock on Atula's door and tell her the phone was for her. If it could wait, I was supposed to get the person's name and number and say that Atula would call back later.

The first couple of days, I was knocking on Atula's door every time the phone rang because everybody said their problem was "REALLY, REALLY URGENT!!!!!!" Atula wasn't too pleased.

"What is the matter with you, Cyril? Can you not see that I am very busy? This is not an urgent call. Now close the door, and please try to use your head in the future."

Andy glared at me like this was some stupid prank I'd dreamed up to bug Atula. Trust me. I had lots of things I'd rather be doing—if anybody would have let me do them. But that didn't seem to dawn on Andy or Atula. So I just rolled my eyes when they weren't looking and started taking messages.

By the end of the day my hand would be all cramped up. Sometimes I'd go through about ten of those pink memo slips for a single message. Nobody ever just said, "It's only me, Darlene Zwicker, calling to see how my divorce papers are coming along." It was always these big long, long stories about all the bad things that had ever happened to them in their entire life. They'd just ramble on and on. "Tell Atula I REALLY got to find out about my petition TODAY because last week Freddie and me was back together and everything was goin' really good so I told her to lay off on the divorce proceedings and all that, then I got my welfare check, eh, and it was gonna pay for the rent and everything because when Freddie and me was havin' our troubles back in March—hold on, no, it wasn't March. It was February. I remember now because he quit drinkin' and everything and—are you gettin' all this?"

Yeah yeah.

I just copied it all down. I'd let Atula figure out what was important and what wasn't.

When I didn't have the phone glued to the side of my head, I had to deal with the clients in the waiting room. People would show up whether they had an appointment or not and just sit around and wait until Atula or Andy could talk to them. By noon the waiting room would be packed, and I know it really stank too, because whenever I ran out for a sub, I'd come back and the smell would hit me like someone had just thrown a big, juicy perspiration-cream pie in my face. No wonder Atula couldn't keep a receptionist.

I don't know how she handled it before Andy kindly volunteered my services, because the place was like that every single day all summer.

Hold on. No, it wasn't. How could I forget? August 20. My birthday. Hardly anybody showed up that day. It was the best present I got—but that's not why they all left me alone. The old Masons' Hall burned down that day. I guess your legal problems don't seem so urgent when there's a big old fire to watch and barbecued bits of people being carted off in ambulances and everything.

But like I said, the office was usually nuts. Sometimes I'd have to break up arguments over who got the last chair or whose turn it was to read the one and only *People Magazine*, but usually I just had to listen.

More sob stories.

More clients demanding to see their attorney "immediately!" (Who do these guys think they are?)

Some people who were really apologetic about not being able to speak English very well, and others who just kept hollering away at me like I was only pretending not to understand Korean.

Students used to come in too, and artists, and this one guy who was writing a screenplay and clearly thought he was too good for us.

And then there were the crazy people.

I'm not just saying crazy the way you say your homeroom teacher or your mother is crazy. These guys were nuts. Like, scary nuts. You know, talking to people who weren't there. Ranting away about how Osama bin Laden was spying on them. Claiming to be Madonna's personal trainer and saying she would be really upset if Atula didn't do something about their problem with the welfare department "RIGHT NOW!!!!!"

I used to make fun of Atula's clients when Andy and I went out for our nightly burger and fries. It seemed perfectly fair to me. These people were ruining my summer. They at least owed me a couple of laughs.

Andy would have a fit, of course. You should have heard her. She'd stick her bottom lip way out and squint her eyes at me and then just let rip. "How could *you*, Cyril Floyd MacIntyre—of all people!—talk about them that way? Has *nothing* I've taught you ever sunk into that THICK SKULL OF YOURS? Do you think these people *choose* to be poor? Huh? Do you? Do you think they *choose* to be sick? Or mentally ill? Or uneducated? Or abused by the system? Huh? Huh? C'mon, answer me, Cyril. ANSWER ME!"

She'd go completely psycho. She'd be spitting food all over the place by the time she got to the part about how people used to look down on her too, pushing a baby carriage at fifteen and not having enough money to cover even "the bare necessities of life." I probably should have known better than to start humming that song from *The Jungle Book* when she said that, but I could never help myself. That's when the "So you think it's funny?" part of the lecture started, and I knew she was going to go at me again until either the manager told her to keep her voice down or she had to go outside for a smoke.

Andy thought her little "chats" were why I stopped making fun of Atula's clients.

Which just goes to show how little she knew about my life.

CHAPTER FIVE

Cruelty
The deliberate infliction of pain

Whenever Andy had to go to the law library or meet a client at the lockup, Atula would send me on some bogus errand near the skateboard bowl. She'd give me twenty bucks for a package of stamps or a box of staples and say, "Keep the change." Then she'd wink and go, "Just make sure you return before your mother does, if you don't mind. I prefer to remain on her good side."

So I'd tell all the regulars to do me a favor and not drive Atula crazy, and I'd take off. I'd pick up my board at the apartment, and a couple of big bottles of root beer at Toulany's, and boot it for the Commons. It didn't matter what day of the week it was or what time of the day, I could always find Kendall there. And since he was there, there were always girls hanging around the skateboard bowl too. But that was just a coincidence—or at least they tried to make it look that way.

I usually checked to see that my hair wasn't completely gross and that my shirt was on right, but I don't think Kendall even noticed the girls. I guess when you're six feet tall and look like he does, you get used to the most popular girls in school following you around.

He'd say "hey" when I showed up, but he wouldn't stop what he was doing. I'd slide down into the bowl, and we'd both work away on our own stuff. He'd do these incredible stunt moves, and I'd just try and stay on my board. We'd only stop when we got really hot. Then we'd lean against that big tree by the jungle gym for a while and chug pop. That's when the girls would move in.

I knew they were all just interested in Kendall, but c'mon! I wasn't going to miss my chance. Not all girls go for the tall, good-looking, cool, athletic guys. For one thing, there aren't that many to go around. And for two, there wouldn't be any skinny, funny, short guys alive today if our skinny, funny, short grandfathers hadn't been able to get a girl now and again. My entire species would have died out.

So I'd start telling Kendall stories in this really loud voice about all the losers who hung around Atula's. He laughed about Darlene and Freddie fighting over who would get the singing-fish trophy when the divorce went through—so all the girls started laughing too. I figured I was golden. Pretty soon they'd all have the hots for me, and I'd have to bribe them to show Kendall a little attention now and then. I just had to keep them laughing long enough that no one noticed I was built like a Chihuahua.

So one day I started telling Kendall about Marge Whynot and her mentally challenged son, Toby, who's, like, thirty and always wants to go feed the duckies. I thought Kendall would find that hilarious, especially when I started doing the whimpering thing Toby does. I was licking my lips and slapping my leg and going, "Please, Mama, pleeeeeease!" and Dorianne and Alexa were killing themselves laughing until Kendall went, "Would you quit it? Would you just lay off?"

I was still thinking I was so funny that it took me a second to realize he meant me. The girls all stopped so fast, I had this feeling I'd just imagined them laughing. I was left standing there with this stupid smile on my face that would have made an amoeba look like a genius in comparison.

I think I said, "Sorry," maybe, or "I was only kidding," and then Kendall said something like, "I just don't find it that funny. He's happy. He likes to feed the ducks. So what?" The girls all looked at Kendall with these big, sad eyes. I knew they were thinking, Not only is he tall, good-looking, athletic and cool—he's really, really sweet too.

They looked at me like I'd just kicked a kitten into oncoming traffic.

I felt like garbage. I couldn't believe what a jerk I was. Like, what kind of pig would make fun of Toby? But Kendall just put his helmet back on like nothing had happened and said, "C'mon. You going to skateboard or what?" We both went back to working on our moves, and he never mentioned it again.

Do you know what the really sad thing is? If Kendall had gone along with my little joke, I'd still be telling Toby stories right now. Anything for a laugh, eh?

How pathetic is that?

CHAPTER SIX

Accusare nemo se debet (Latin)
A legal principle meaning no one is required to say
anything to incriminate himself or herself

John Hugh Gillis still reeked and was still lying about
where he was on the night of September 17. Elmore
Himmelman still gave me the creeps, and frankly,
I thought he'd be better off in a mental hospital than
out on the streets, screaming at people who weren't
there and scaring the people who were. Darlene
and Freddie still drove me crazy. Stay married or get
divorced. I didn't care what they did—I just wanted
them to make up their minds and leave us alone.

But after that thing with Kendall down at the
skateboard bowl, I wasn't such a jerk about Atula's
other clients. I'm not saying I'd want to hang out
with any of them—except maybe Mr. Lucas, who
was pretty funny for an old guy—but I sort of got

to like them in a take 'em-or-leave 'em kind of way. Most of them were pretty nice. Nicer than me, that's for sure. I mean, I felt really bad about Toby and Marge, especially when they came in with Timbits for everybody one day. I knew they didn't have any money—that's why they were at Atula's, to get more money from the government—but they went out and spent $4.98 on Tim's jumbo variety pack so none of their "friends down to the law office" would go hungry. I felt even worse because I had a bag of jujubes in my top drawer that I didn't plan on sharing.

Andy noticed that I was better with the clients and started talking about how I'd "matured" over the summer. She said it in a way that made it sound like she was this really fantastic parent—as if *she* had something to do with it—and that bugged me so much that I almost told her about Kendall. I would have loved to see her face when she found out I'd only "matured" because Kendall, the guy she hated, thought I was being a jerk. But I wasn't that dumb. Tell Andy about Kendall, and she'd know that Atula had let me go down to the bowl, that I'd been lying to her and, most important, that I was actually managing to have a little fun that summer. She couldn't let that happen.

So I just kept my mouth shut. Things were going pretty good. Andy had the perfect job (she got paid to argue with people). I had some freedom. We had some money.

Too bad things didn't stay that way.

CHAPTER SEVEN

Malpractice

The failure to perform professional services competently

We were playing Scrabble one night, and even though I was seriously beating her, Andy was in a really good mood. She'd just been to the official opening of this new Immigration Resource Center. She was making it sound like she was so happy because the center was finally built. Because needy people would finally have a place to go, someone to help them.

Yeah right.

If that was her only reason, how come Andy was going on and on about her and Atula being driven there personally by the center's honorary chair and getting to sit at the head table and having him thank her by name in his little speech and blah, blah, blah?

I'll tell you why.

Because it made her feel important. Like she was a big shot. A VIP (which, of course, she was— very insane person). Can't you just imagine how much Andy loved stepping out of the guy's big green BMW just as James Monihan and those other stuck-up dorks from her law-school class were arriving at the ceremony? It must have been one of the best things that ever happened to her. James goes to work at some fancy law firm while Andy goes to work at Atula's, but she's the one pulling up in a BMW! Life doesn't get much better than that.

I knew that's what she was thinking, but I pretended I didn't. I nodded at all the right places and acted like I was interested—then, when she least expected it, I put *defunct* down on a triple word score. Eighty-nine points, not counting the ten I got for turning *ax* into *tax*. She might have got to sit at the head table, but that didn't matter to the Undisputed King of Scrabble.

That sure wiped the smile off her face. There was no way she was going to catch up now. Unless, of course, she cheated.

Suddenly she was insisting that I go check the mailbox immediately.

I knew it was only so she could see what other letters were left in the bag, and I said so. She, of course, was appalled.

Cheat?

Andy?

Why, it was the furthest thing from her mind! She'd just forgotten to look in the mailbox that day, and she needed to find out if the War Amps had sent her keys back yet.

That sure wiped the smile off my face.

I couldn't believe it. Andy had lost another stupid set of keys! She was worse than a kid. She was so disorganized! What was the matter with her? She was always losing things, forgetting stuff, making a mess of our life. How was she ever going to be a real lawyer if she couldn't keep track of anything?

I'm not kidding. It's serious. If a lawyer loses a piece of evidence or forgets to file a document by a certain time or doesn't show up at a hearing, she can get in really big trouble. She can lose her case. She can get sued for malpractice. She can screw up bad enough that she gets disbarred and can't work as a lawyer anymore.

I knew it was just a set of keys, but it really worried me. I didn't want Andy to mess up again.

I didn't want to go back to her babysitting and being unhappy all the time.

I didn't want to go back to us being just this juvenile-delinquent mother and her loser kid.

I knew if she saw my face she'd know exactly what I was thinking, and I really didn't want to get into that with her right then. I took the bag of Scrabble tiles—so she couldn't pick out the good letters—and went to check the mail.

I opened the door to our apartment and practically swallowed my tongue. There was this long-haired guy right in front of me with his hand in our mailbox.

CHAPTER EIGHT

Tampering with the mail

An offense under the Criminal Code

The guy was probably as surprised as I was, but he just went, "Hey. Yo," like it was no big deal to be rooting through someone else's mail.

I said, "What do you think you're doing?" Andy was in the kitchen, so I could sound as tough as I wanted.

He gave this big smile, and I knew right away that he considered himself a very charming guy. "Oh, sorry, man. Just making sure I was in the right place." He handed me the War Amps envelope like he was doing me a favor and said, "Did you lose your keys?"

I rolled my eyes. Did he really think that if he just kept talking, I'd forget he was trying to steal our mail?

I guess so.

He kept yammering on. "Great little service the war amputees provide, eh? You buy a tag from them for your key chain. You lose your keys. Somebody finds them, throws them into any old mailbox, and the War Amps sends them back to you! You get your keys, and some poor guy without an arm or a leg gets some help. Pretty amazing, eh?"

I shook my head and snorted to show what a jerk he was. "Ever think of doing a commercial for them?" I said, all sarcastic. "You'd make a great spokesmodel."

He laughed at that. "Matter of fact, I have," he said. "I haven't introduced myself. Byron Cuvelier."

He stuck his right hand out at me to shake.

That's when I realized he didn't have a right hand.

CHAPTER NINE

Alias (Latin)
A false name

All he had was this kind of lumpy, purplish stump that ended where his wrist should have started. I could see all the scars where it had been stitched up. I felt like a complete nosehole. As bad as when I made fun of Toby.

Byron, on the other hand—if you'll pardon the pun—was having a great time. "Oh, sorry," he went. "I guess I left my hand in my other jacket." Then he kind of jabbed the stump at me, and I jumped back. That killed him. "Worried I was going to pinch you or something?" Ha-ha. "I don't pinch too good since I lost my fingers."

I sort of smiled and went heh-heh. I figured I had to be nice since I'd been such a jerk about that spokesmodel thing. He said, "Is Squeaky in?"

Squeaky?

"No," I said. "You got the wrong place." Thank God.

"Don't think I do," he said and gave me a big *Entertainment Tonight* smile. Is there anything more pathetic than some guy in his thirties who thinks he's a rock star?

"Ah…sorry," I said. "Only me and my mother live here."

"I know," he said, "and I want to talk to her. So be a good boy—"

Did I hate this guy or what?

"—and go get Squeaky for me."

By this time I wasn't feeling bad about the spokesmodel line anymore. I just wanted to get rid of this piece of garbage.

"Trust me," I said. "There's no Squeaky here. See?"

I turned around and yelled, "Squeaky! Hey, Squeeeeeak-y! You have a gentleman caller!" I looked at Byron and laughed. I was just dying to see what Andy would do to him.

I didn't have to wait long. Andy came flying down the hall and grabbed me with both arms. She squashed my face into her neck. I could feel her shaking.

She whispered, "How'd you find me, Cuvelier?"

CHAPTER TEN

Intimidation
Using violence or threats to make a person do—or not do—something

"Where there's a will, Blue Eyes, there's a way."

Oh, barf. Byron was really turning on the charm. It was gross—and it wasn't working either.

"DON'T CALL ME BLUE EYES!" Andy screamed, and a bit of spit splattered on his cheesy, fake-leather jacket.

"Okay, Squeaky."

"DON'T CALL ME SQUEAKY!"

Byron shrugged as if he was only trying his best to please her.

"I'm not sure what to call you anymore, darlin'. Ann? Angela? Andrea? MacKenzie? MacLeod? MacIntyre? What's your pleasure?"

She blew up. "My pleasure is that you get your [*beep*]ing [*beep*] out of here and stay the [*beep*] away from me and my [*beep*]ing kid. If I ever see that [*beep*]ing ugly face of yours again, I'm going to call the [*beep*]ing cops."

Byron wasn't going anywhere. He just looked down at his shoes for a second and came up laughing. "Well now, I wouldn't do that if I was you. You never know what the police might think about a parent talking that way in front of a young child—'specially a parent with your, ahhh, history."

Andy went maroon. I was just waiting for her to blow up again. She didn't say anything for a really long time. Then she looked at me and said, "Cyril, go to your room, turn the radio up high, and shut the door."

I was wild. I wanted to stay and find out what happened next. "Oh, come on!" I said, but she screamed, "NOW!" and I knew I'd better just shut up and do what I was told.

I tried to hear what they were talking about, but I couldn't, not when they were whispering and I had to keep the music up so loud. I tried to record their voices with the pathetic little spy recorder I got for my eleventh birthday, but the batteries were dead. I tried to sneak out into the hall, but she caught me, and honest to God, I thought she was going to kill me right there.

So even now I don't know exactly what they said to each other. All I know is that twenty minutes later Byron had moved into my room, and I was sleeping on the couch.

CHAPTER ELEVEN

Harassment
Unsolicited words or conduct meant to annoy, alarm or abuse another person

Things kind of tanked after that. I started eighth grade a couple of weeks later. Byron never left the house. And Andy was in a rotten mood all the time. She'd never say a thing to Byron when I was around, but she stayed up late every night hissing at him. I couldn't hear what they were saying, but I could tell by the tone of her voice that it wasn't good.

Her diet and her smoking were getting worse too. Maybe it was the stress, but I thought it was more likely she was just doing it to bug Byron. And if that was her plan, I was 100 percent behind her. What a guy. He, like, moves in with us, kicks me out of my room—and then starts complaining about second-hand smoke and our unhealthy eating habits.

Like we wanted him there.

Like we cared what he thought.

Like we could afford to eat better with him scrounging off us.

So Andy smoked in his face all the time just to make her point—i.e., "you can leave any time." Of course, she would have made the point a whole lot better if she'd stopped paying for his takeout organic salads every night, but would she listen to me?

On top of that, Andy was screwing up at Atula's too. I figured it was because of all those late nights arguing with Byron, but she wouldn't tell me much about it. I'd just catch bits and pieces when I met her at her office after work. One night—about three weeks after Byron parked his carcass in my room—I was coming to get Andy to go to McDonald's and I heard Atula really laying into her. I guess Andy had rolled her eyes at a judge in court that day—not something you do if you're actually hoping to win your case—and Atula was ripping. She was going on about this being the last straw, about Andy's bad attitude lately, about being tired of having to cover for all Andy's sloppy mistakes, etc., etc., etc. I had the feeling Atula was just getting started, but I'll never know. She saw me at the top of the stairs and stopped talking immediately.

That was bad.

I knew Atula. She wasn't usually scared to say things in front of me. All I could think was that Andy must be in really big trouble for her to shut up like that.

Atula fiddled with the scarf she always wears and then said something like, "You two must be hungry. Why don't you toddle off for dinner, and we can discuss this at another time?"

Andy sat on the curb outside McDonald's, sucking on her, like, twenty-third cigarette, while I went inside and grabbed two Big Mac combos. We headed home. She wouldn't eat, and she wouldn't talk. She wouldn't even say "None of your business" like she usually did when I tried to find out what the deal was with Byron. She wouldn't say anything.

We got back to the apartment, and Byron was his usual charming self, asking about school and work like he was a regular Mr. Mom. That took guts. Andy looked at him like he was one of those slimy hair boogers that clog up the shower drain. He said, "Anyone ever tell you how gorgeous you are when you're mad?" She went into the kitchen and slammed the door.

That meant I was stuck with Byron. There was no way I was going to go into the kitchen with Andy looking the way she did. (Byron was the one who had pissed her off, but that didn't mean she wouldn't take it out on me.) I couldn't go into my bedroom because it was Byron's bedroom now, and he wasn't leaving the living room. I thought for a minute of going out and finding Kendall, but I couldn't do that either. I mean, I wouldn't have felt good about leaving Andy all alone with Stumpy, the One-Armed Nosehole. So I sat as far away from him as I could on our one and only couch and tried to watch TV.

Just my luck that Byron was feeling chatty. He looked at me like we were finally getting a chance to have a little man-to-man talk.

As if either of us qualified.

I ignored him. I just stared at the screen while he yakked away.

For a guy who thought he was so smooth, he always managed to say the wrong thing. I was starting to think it wasn't an accident.

"What grade are you in?"

I shouldn't have answered him. I knew I shouldn't have answered him.

He went, "Graa-aa-ade eight? I thought you were, like, eleven!"

Yeah, and I thought you were, like, human, but only for a minute there.

"Or even ten. Lord liftin'! You're some puny for grade eight! I keep telling your mother she should feed you better."

I wish your mother hadn't fed you at all.

"Hey, what's that look for? Gee, didn't mean to offend you or nothin.' I bet all the girls think you're pretty cute actually. Girls love the little guys. You're like bunnies or kittens or something to them. Must bring out their maternal instincts, I guess."

Yeah, and you bring out my killer instinct.

"Not much of a talker, are you?…

"Maybe you're more the physical type…

"Wanna arm-wrestle then?"

No, I don't want to arm-wrestle. Because that would mean I'd have to touch you, and call me a wuss, but slimy reptiles have always kind of given me the creeps— no offense.

"C'mon! You're not scared, are ya?"

Yeah right. Me? Scared of a fingerless stump? I don't think so. Grossed out? Yes. Sick of seeing it waving around in my face? Absolutely. But scared? Think again. I'll even prove it.

"Sure," I finally said. "I'll arm-wrestle you."

Byron took off that cheesy jacket he always wore, and I wished I'd just kept my big mouth shut. He actually looked pretty strong. One of those lean-mean-fighting-machine types. Even the arm without a hand was all pumped.

He saw me looking and said, "Hundred and fifty push-ups a day is all it takes. Pretty good, eh, for an amputee." He grabbed his wrist and made his muscles pop.

I pretended it was nothing special. I said, "Oh, please. I was just looking at your tattoos. Maybe if you hadn't wasted so much money on them, you wouldn't have to be mooching meals off a single mother."

He laughed and said, "You sure are smart for a little fella," and I knew I had to beat him. He put his right elbow on the old packing crate we use as a coffee table, and I grabbed the stump with my hand. There was a squishy bit on the top that was really gross. He had one ounce of fat on his entire body, and it just so happened to be the part I had to grab on to.

He said, "One, two, three, go," and the match was over. Byron flattened me. It was pathetic.

He said, "Sorry," which he wasn't, then, "What say we even things up here a bit? You try her with both arms this time."

I was going to say something like "bite me," but I knew it was the only chance I had. I said, "Whatever" and grabbed the stump with both hands.

He said, "One, two, three, go." I saw the big dove tattoo on his biceps twitch, and then he slammed my arms against the packing crate. My head hit the edge of the couch, and I saw stars.

Really.

For about thirty seconds there were these little white twinkly things dancing around in front of me. I used to think they were only in cartoons.

Byron was smoothing down that armpitty little beard of his so I wouldn't see him laughing. I pretended I didn't notice and said, "Those are the ugliest tattoos I've ever seen." It was true, though that's not why I said it. His arms were covered with peace signs and that hippie black-and-white circle thing and hearts with initials in them and then the worst—this big red rose with *Yours for all time* written over it.

"You're a regular love machine," I said and made this face like I was going to barf.

"Yeah, well, some people know what's important in life and some people don't," he said. "Okay, Mr. Schwarzenegger, try it with my bad arm now." He put his left elbow on the table, and I saw there was this big red blistery thing above his wrist. He saw me looking.

"See what happens? Jessica, my old girlfriend, didn't know what was important, and I had to get her tattoo burned right off."

"Gee, that must have broken her heart," I said and grabbed his hand with both of mine.

This time I had a chance. I started pulling with all my might, and I saw the C.C. tattoo on the inside of his arm bulge. He tried to keep yammering away as if this was nothing, but he was straining. He. Talked. Like. This. He said, "I remember. When your mother. Knew what was important." I got up on one foot and pushed as hard as I could.

He went, "Her and me. Used to have some times. Back then." I was standing right up now and using all my body weight against him, and I didn't care that it was cheating. He was starting to pant. He said, "Once. When she was about. Sixteen, we—"

That was the last I heard. Andy came tearing out of the kitchen, screeching at him to "shut the [beep] up!"

Ooh, that made me mad. I'd almost won. And I'd almost found out what was going on. But Andy wasn't going to let that happen. She screamed at Byron. And then she screamed at me to brush my teeth and go to bed.

I didn't argue. I knew by the color of her face that it wouldn't get me anywhere. I told her I needed to get a T-shirt from my dresser and left her giving Byron the evil eye. I went into my old room, grabbed my spy recorder from under the bed and wrapped it in a clean T-shirt. I went into the bathroom and locked the door. I brushed my teeth with the battery-operated toothbrush the dentist thought might help with my cavities. Then I sat on the toilet and peed. I needed to sit so I could take the batteries out of the toothbrush and put them in the spy recorder. If I took too long in the bathroom, Andy would be suspicious. I put on the T-shirt, threw my jeans in the laundry hamper and hid the spy recorder inside my boxers. Then I took my jeans out of the hamper and left them on the floor. Be too neat and Andy would be suspicious about that too.

I went into the kitchen and hid the recorder on the table behind a pile of advertising flyers, school bulletins and junk like that. Andy screamed at me from the living room, "What are you doing in there, Cyril? I told you, it's time for bed!"

I screamed back, "Can't a guy have a drink of water? Geez!" I turned on the tap and made a big deal of clanking around in the cupboard for a glass. I drank a bit, left the half-empty glass on the counter and went into the living room.

"How can I go to bed with you guys in here?" I said, like I was really PO'ed. "Do you think you could carry on this discussion in the kitchen perhaps—or would that be too much to ask?"

Byron said, "I can't believe you let him mouth off to you like that," which, of course, was the only reason Andy did.

She said, "Don't tell me how to raise my kid." She banged her face into my forehead, which I suppose was a kiss goodnight. Then they went into the kitchen and shut the door.

I couldn't hear anything they said, but that didn't bother me. I'd pick up the spy recorder the next day after Andy went to work. I could usually count on Byron to spend at least half an hour in the shower, especially if I acted like I needed to pee.

I went to sleep thinking I was a genius. A regular James Bond.

CHAPTER TWELVE

Interception

Anyone who, by means of any electromagnetic, acoustic, mechanical or other device, willfully intercepts a private communication is guilty of an indictable offense and liable to imprisonment for a term not exceeding five years

A DOOR SLAMS. A CHAIR SQUEAKS ACROSS THE FLOOR. FINGERS TAP ON THE TABLE. PAPERS RUSTLE. SOMEONE PACES BACK AND FORTH.

BYRON: (SINGING) Love. Love will keep us together. Dee da doodoo da dee doo.

A PLATE SMASHES. THEN ANOTHER. FOOTSTEPS FOLLOW.

BYRON: Ooh. Temper, temper!

SOMETHING THUMPS THE TABLE. GLASSES RATTLE.

ANDY: What the [beep] do you think you're doing?

BYRON: Singin'. You used to like my voice.

ANDY: Don't get smart with me! You know what I mean. What were you saying to Cyril?

BYRON: Nothin'. I was just reminiscin'!

ANDY: Well, don't.

BYRON: Oh, come on. He was gettin' right into it!

ANDY: [Beep]

BYRON: Seems there's a lot about his mother and me he don't know.

ANDY: Yeah. And I want to keep it that way.

BYRON: Well, this is what I've been tryin' to tell you all along, darlin'! That can be arranged. All I'm asking for is a little quid pro quo. You know—you scratch my back, I'll scratch yours.

ANDY: Quid. Pro. Quo. (LAUGHS) Well, aren't you the [beep]ing legal scholar.

BYRON: Yup. Jail time will do that to you.

A LOUD NOISE—POSSIBLY SOMEONE KICKING THE WALL—IS FOLLOWED BY A LONG PAUSE.

ANDY: You're not going to let me forget that, are you?

BYRON: Hey, somebody's got to keep you humble. Big-city lawyer… Too good for her old friends…

ANDY: Shut up! SHUT UP! Look. I was a kid. I made a mistake, a huge [*beep*]ing mistake! And I am sorry!

BYRON: Well, here's your chance to do something about it.

ANDY: HOW MANY TIMES DO I HAVE TO TELL YOU? I can't! Even if I believed you, there's nothing I can do.

BYRON: Yes, there is. I got everything you need to take him down.

ANDY: So you do it then.

BYRON: Yeah, right. You're just tryin' to get rid of me.

ANDY: Bingo!

BYRON: I guess it worked for you before.

ANDY: [*Beep*].

TWENTY-SECOND PAUSE

ANDY: Why the [*beep*] me? Why don't you go to somebody else?

BYRON: I don't trust anybody else.

ANDY: You? Trust me? What are you, nuts?

BYRON: No. Logical.

ANDY: Now he thinks he's [*beep*]ing Socrates.

BRYON: I know I can count on you.

ANDY: Oh, right. And how do you know that?

BYRON: Because we both need something from each other.

ANDY: I don't need anything from you!

BYRON: Yes, you do, baby doll.

ANDY: DON'T CALL ME BA—

BYRON: (INTERRUPTING) You need me to keep my mouth shut. And I will, 'cause you know how much I'd hate to have to tell Cyril the truth about his dear old mother.

ANDY: YOU [BEEP]ING [BEEP BEEP BEEP BEEP]! That's my choice? Ruin my career or ruin my life?

BYRON: Think of it as a chance to do something good for someone else.

ANDY: [Beep] off. I've looked after you for weeks. That's good enough.

BYRON: Hey, it's not for me! It's for my friend. You know, the dead guy.

ANDY: Yeah. Right. *It's not for me!* You expect me to believe that? You just want revenge.

BYRON: Can you blame me? It's about time I got something out of this deal.

ANDY: (SUSTAINED CURSING. BARELY AUDIBLE.)

FINGERNAILS CLICK AGAINST THE TABLE.

THE SOUND OF A LIGHTER FLICKING IS FOLLOWED BY AN INTAKE OF BREATH AND A LOUD SIGH.

BYRON: (COUGHING)
ANDY: What do I have to do?
BYRON: Put out that cigarette and I'll tell you.
ANDY: [Beep] off. This is my apartment.
BYRON: And these are my lungs.

THIRTY-SECOND PAUSE

BYRON: Okay. I'm a reasonable man.
ANDY: Oooooooh, right!
BYRON: You can smoke outside.
ANDY: Fine.
BYRON: (COUGHING) Do you mind not blowing it right in my face?

CHAIRS SQUEAK ACROSS THE FLOOR. A DOOR OPENS AND SLAMS SHUT.

SILENCE.

CHAPTER THIRTEEN

Truancy
Unexcused absence from school

I made it through history class the next day, but I couldn't hack it after that. I had to get out of school. I needed to think. When the bell rang for second period, I snuck out the back door and over the parking-lot fence.

Kendall had moved to another school. I thought about trying to catch him at lunch, but what was I going to say? We'd never really talked about private stuff before, and I thought I should maybe ease him into it. You know, ask him what his father did, for example, or tell him I was afraid of spiders or that I wet my bed until I was eleven. See how he handled that before hitting him with some story about my mother being blackmailed into doing something illegal by this homeless ex-convict.

It was sort of a lot to dump on him out of the blue like that.

And anyway, what could Kendall do about it? Lend me that fancy new skateboard of his? Introduce me to some hot girls? Show me how to do a kick-flip? That would take my mind off the problem for a while, but in the end, Andy would still be in trouble.

I decided to pretend I was sick and go home. Maybe I could get Byron in a chatty mood again.

I was just coming round the corner on Cornwallis Street when I saw Byron. I couldn't believe it. He'd lived with us for almost a month and hadn't left the apartment once—at least that I knew of.

It was pretty clear he didn't want anybody else to know about this little excursion. He wasn't dressed in a disguise exactly, but he didn't look like himself. I only knew who it was because I saw him walking out the door of our building. His stump was tucked into his pocket. He was wearing this old jacket that Andy had picked up in the men's department of the Salvation Army ages ago. It was way too big for her, but she used to think it looked pretty cool. He was wearing a ballcap, and I thought at first he'd tucked his hair up under it. I got a better look when he turned onto Gottingen Street, and I realized what he'd done. He'd cut off his hair and that weaselly beard of his too. He looked practically presentable.

I followed him. He was walking pretty fast and keeping his eyes on the sidewalk. Still, I had to be careful he didn't see me. It wasn't all that easy. There's not a whole bunch of trees in our part of town. I kept about half a block behind him and had to do quite a bit of darting around. Byron might not have looked suspicious, but I sure did.

He walked past where all the stores were and turned up this quiet little street. There was no traffic and no people to hide behind, so I had to hang back. I let him turn the corner, waited a couple of minutes and tried to catch up.

I got to the top of the street but couldn't see him anywhere. I didn't know whether to go left down the street or right up the street or straight ahead into this sad-looking little church. People in old movies always have their secret meetings in churches, but somehow I couldn't see it working for Byron. If I were the minister and I saw Byron in my church, I'd start worrying about the collection money. I'd call the police immediately.

So I ruled out the church and decided to turn right because, well, I had to do something. I couldn't just stand there.

I hadn't gone very far—maybe ten, fifteen steps—when I suddenly realized that Byron was sitting on a park bench right across the street from me. I would have seen him sooner except I'd been daydreaming. You know, imagining myself on CNN, talking about how I single-handedly caught this master criminal, instead of actually trying to catch him. It would have been funny if it wasn't so sad.

I dove behind a parked car and just sat there shaking for a while. I was really scared that Byron had seen me and was going to come over and pound my lights out with that purple stump of his.

I waited, but nothing happened. I decided that I was going to crawl back to the corner and make a run for home.

It seemed like the sensible thing to do, but it was too pathetic even for me. I could just see me slithering along on my belly right when Mary MacIsaac happened by. It wouldn't be long before everyone at school heard that not only was I mean to the mentally challenged, but I was a chicken too. That would pretty much have killed any chance I had to get a girl in this lifetime.

I decided to stay and find out what was going on. After all, there was Andy to think about too. I peeked up through the car windshield. Byron was still there.

He was sitting on a bench in this little tiny park, talking to a woman. A small dark-haired woman with a big bandage on her arm. Her back was to me, but she was moving her hands around a lot, so I could tell she was talking. I could tell she was upset. Byron was doing his chick-magnet thing and patting her on the leg. She seemed to calm down a bit (the hands weren't flying around quite as much), but then Andy showed up. The little woman practically jumped into Byron's arms.

As soon as she turned around, I knew exactly who she was.

Consuela Rodriguez.

CHAPTER FOURTEEN

In camera (Latin)
The hearing of a case in private

It probably sounds funny that I remember her, because she only came into Atula's office once last summer, and she was really quiet too. But that kind of made her stand out. Sort of like those teachers who, instead of screaming at the class to quiet down, start whispering. In a weird way, it gets your attention even better.

I remembered Consuela didn't speak English. The only things she could say were "Atula?" (which I guess isn't English) and "Do you talk Spanish?" which of course I didn't.

I remembered her name because it had taken me, like, half an hour to figure out what she was saying.

Onsweda?

Consweera?

Consweto?

Rodreekays?

Rotrigaze?

Rodrinkhaze?

She'd been really patient and nice about it, but she finally just took my little message pad and wrote the name herself. Then she smiled and went and stood in the back of the room. She waited all day. Sometime in the afternoon she managed to score a chair. By four thirty there were only a couple of people left, and even though she didn't have an appointment—who did?— she had a really good chance of seeing Atula that day.

At about five Atula came out of her office and asked me if some man had called her. It was the sort of question Atula asked all the time. The name didn't mean anything to me. I wouldn't even have remembered her saying it, except that when I did, Consuela bolted. She knocked a chair over on her way out. It made this huge racket. We all kind of stopped and looked. Atula asked me who she was, and I told her. Atula shrugged as if she'd never heard of her and went back to her office. I crumpled up the pink paper with Consuela's name on it and slam-dunked it into the wastepaper basket.

That must have been sometime in late August, I guess. Consuela had never crossed my mind again until this moment in the park.

I was dying to find out what she was saying, but I couldn't hear from where I was, and there was no way I could get any closer. There was just the car and wide open space between us. All I could do was watch through the windshield.

Too bad I can't lip-read. They were there for about an hour, but I still didn't have a clue what was going on. Consuela talked. Byron talked. Andy said things every so often, but mostly she just scribbled stuff down on a big yellow legal pad.

At about eleven Byron said something, and suddenly the meeting was all over. I managed to get my head down about a nanosecond before they started coming right for me.

I slid under the car and prayed.

As they got closer, I started to make out what they were saying. Andy said something about having to get going. Then Consuela went, "Thank...you... for...my...ummm...ahhhh."

She said something in Spanish, and Byron said, "Children."

Consuela said, "Thank you for my cheeldren, Hhhhandy."

Andy just said, "Yeah, okay." Byron and Consuela kept talking away in Spanish. The only words I could make out were *adios*, when they left, and *Carlos*, because they said it, like, ten times, and that's the name of the guy in the Bonanza Burritos commercial. ("Who can eat another? Carlos can!")

Andy left by the little side street. By the sound of their footsteps, I guessed that Consuela and Byron were headed back downtown. I stayed under the car until I was sure they were gone. In fact, I stayed under the car until the guy who owned it came out and said, "What are you doing under my car? Get outta there! Don't you know you can get yourself killed that way? Damn kid! What's the matter with you?"

I almost told him.

CHAPTER FIFTEEN

Fraud

Deceitful conduct designed to manipulate another person to give up something of value

Things had changed since I'd listened to my spy recorder on the way to school that morning. I still felt like throwing up, but for different reasons. I'd thought at first that my mother had gotten herself messed up with some really bad guy. Now I thought she'd gotten herself messed up with some really smart bad guy. Byron spoke Spanish as easily as he spoke English. Not just anyone could do that.

There was also something about his whole...I don't know, manner, I guess. The guy didn't have any money or any job or any big fat title, but he still walked around like he owned the place. Like he was in charge. It was kind of creepy. Like, what was this? Mind control or something? What did he have over everybody? Why wasn't everybody just telling him to get lost? Why wasn't *anybody*?

The Consuela thing was weird too. I didn't know her—like I said, I'd only seen her that one time—but she sure hadn't seemed like your typical criminal. She'd seemed sweet and nice and kind of scared of everything. Maybe that was just some big act, but I have to tell you, she had me convinced.

I started to think that maybe Byron was blackmailing both of them. About what, I didn't know. All I knew was that Byron was beginning to look more like an evil genius and less like some dirty bum who'd kicked me out of my bedroom.

I needed some time to pull myself together. I found this playground nobody I know goes to and sat on a swing until I got cold and some little kid started hassling me about hogging it. Then I hung out at Toulany's for a couple of hours, until the guy behind the counter pointed at the No Loitering sign and told me to buy something or get going. I bought one red licorice. He rolled his eyes, and I left. It was almost six o'clock by this time, and I knew that if I didn't get home soon, Andy would be suspicious. I'd just say I'd stayed late for science club or some other dorky thing.

I tried to come into the apartment the same way I always did. I threw the door open so it banged against the wall. I dumped my backpack right in the middle of the floor so Andy would have to kick it out of her way when she walked in. And then I got all ready not to answer when Byron did his "How was school?" thing.

Only problem was, Byron didn't do anything. Didn't say anything either. The apartment was dead quiet.

I went to the bathroom as if I needed to pee. I went to the kitchen as if I was hoping there might be some leftover pizza. I stuck my head in my old room as if I was looking for my sneakers.

Byron wasn't anywhere.

That's okay, I thought. He knows I'll be back from school by now. He'll have an excuse all ready for why a homebody like him would be out on the town. I even figured out what I was going to say when he walked in: "Hey, I thought vampires weren't allowed out in daylight." It was a little lame, but it was good enough.

I could see there was a message on the phone, and I realized that Mrs. Payzant had probably called to find out why I hadn't been in school. I figured Andy had her on the payroll. Mrs. Payzant was always really nice to my face, but as soon as I came in three minutes late or got less than 99.4 percent on a test, she was calling Andy to discuss her "concerns." Between the two of them, they'd pretty much killed any chance I had to be normal.

I was right. Mrs. Payzant had called. I just had to hope it had been after Byron left. I erased her message and listened to the next one. It had come in at 3:38 PM. It was from Andy.

"Hello, honey," she said. "It's just me, Mama. I'm going to be home a little late for dinner, but I made you something and put it in the freezer. If you want to get yourself some of those donuts you like—you know, the ones with the special filling—there's some money in the Player's tobacco tin by the stove. I'll be back as soon as I can. Oh, and if you need to reach me, call me at—"

The line went dead, but I had heard enough to know what had happened.

An alien had taken over my mother's mouth.

CHAPTER SIXTEEN

Dismissal
Termination of employment; the firing of an
employee

Honey?!?

Mama?!?

I made you something?!?

What was going on? What happened to "Hey,
kid, it's me. Meet ya at McDonald's in fifteen. There's
a coupon on the fridge for a free burger"?

And what was that thing about special donuts?
I didn't even like donuts. She was the one who liked
donuts.

Was this a joke? Nah. Andy could never make
it through one of her own jokes without cracking
up.

Was she trying to impress someone? Act like the
perfect mother? If that's what she was trying to do,
she'd kind of blown it. Perfect mothers don't usually

leave money in Player's tobacco tins, because perfect mothers don't usually roll their own cigarettes.

Normally I met Andy around six thirty for dinner, but I couldn't wait. I had to find out what this was all about.

I called the office. I got Atula. She was wild.

"No, Cyril, I regret that your mother is not in. She has not been in all day. In fact, I just received a telephone call from a colleague of mine. A very important colleague. Andy missed a meeting with him and as a result may have jeopardized future expansion of the Immigration Resource Center. He is not the least bit happy about it, I assure you, and neither am I. I am very sorry to have to tell you this, Cyril, but as of today, Andy no longer works for Varma and Associates."

I didn't know what to say. I just sort of went, "Oh…right…okay…yeah." I didn't even want to think about what this meant. Andy might be a little late for a meeting or forget papers she needed or file them under *Deveau* instead of *Devine*. But she never missed a meeting. She was really serious about work. She wouldn't screw up something as important to her as the Immigration Center just because she was too lazy or pissed off or freaked out by a little black-mail to show up when she was supposed to.

I knew right then that something really, really bad had happened.

I couldn't stay on the phone anymore. I mumbled something about having to go, but Atula wouldn't let me off that easy.

"There's one more thing I'd like to say to you, Cyril."

Oh, *geeez*, I thought. Now what?

"I want you to know that my quarrel with your mother has nothing to do with you. You are a bright, capable boy, and I very much appreciated your help in the office this summer. You know, or at least I hope you know, that you are always welcome here. If you ever need help—or even just a home-cooked meal for a change—you should come to me. I make a very good chicken curry. Do you understand, Cyril?" Pause.

"Cyril?"

I didn't know what to say. "Thanks?" Or "As a matter of fact, I could use some help?"

In the end, I just said thanks.

CHAPTER SEVENTEEN

Abandonment

Failure to provide the necessaries of life for a minor child

I stayed up all that night. There was no way I could sleep. I went back and forth between being really, really scared and being ready to kill Andy. What was she thinking? Why had she even let Byron stay with us in the first place?!? Obviously, something terrible is going to happen if you let a jerk like that into your life.

At eight thirty the next morning I washed my face and changed my shirt. I left a note in the hall. *COME AND GET ME AT SCHOOL AS SOON AS YOU GET HOME!!!!!* I grabbed my backpack and left.

I didn't know where Andy was. I didn't know what she'd done or why she'd done it or what I should do about it.

All I knew was that nobody could find out she was gone.

I know what you're thinking. You're thinking, What?!? Are you nuts? She could be in trouble! Call the cops!

But it wasn't that easy.

Call the cops, and they'd find out I was thirteen and living alone. Then what would they do? They'd send me to a foster home. They'd have no other choice. It's not like I had any relatives who wanted me.

It's not like I had *anybody* who wanted me.

Then the cops would start trying to find Andy, and I was really afraid of what they'd find her doing. The best possibility, believe it or not, was that Byron was forcing her to do something she shouldn't. I remembered from law school that if you commit a crime "under duress," you can use that as a defense.

You know, an excuse.

In other words, you can say to the judge, "It's not my fault! He made me do it!" and if you're lucky, the judge will believe you and let you off.

Like I said, if you're lucky.

But there's no counting on the judge believing you. Especially if you're Andy. With our luck, she'd get the judge she'd rolled her eyes at.

What I was really worried about was that Andy would get a taste of her old wild ways again and start liking them. I mean, she'd given up smoking before. She'd made a big deal about how much better she felt and how much more money we had and how she'd "never smoke another butt ever again, so help me God." And, well, you know what happened with that. Why wouldn't she take up getting in trouble again? She obviously used to like it. She did it for years.

I didn't know much about her life on the street, and I knew why I didn't. Andy didn't want it getting out. Why would she? It was hard enough for her to pull off the "responsible citizen" act without every-body knowing about her juvie record.

God. I hated to think what kind of stuff she must have gotten into back then.

If I sicced the cops on Andy and they found her doing something illegal, our life would be ruined. If she got convicted of a crime, she could get kicked out of the legal profession. On top of everything, she could even be charged with abandoning me. "Failing to provide the necessaries of life for a minor child," they call it. She used to joke about that when I was little. I'd have a fit because she wouldn't buy me some action figure or some remote-control car we couldn't afford, and she'd go, "What are you going to do, Cyril? Charge me? I hate to break it to you, kid, but under the law, Super Thunderwheel Mini SUVs aren't considered a 'necessary of life.'"

It wasn't a joke this time. Unless Andy had a really good excuse for taking off, she could lose custody of me. For good.

Andy could lose me. She could lose her job. She could go to jail.

I had no other choice. I had to find her myself.

I got to school, and Mrs. Payzant asked where I'd been. I said I had the flu. She said I still looked pale (no kidding). Was I feeling all right?

I said no, and I meant it. She said I should go home then. There was a terrible bug going around. Her son had been in bed for ten days. Why didn't she call my mother at the office to come and get me?

I said that my mother didn't go in to the office today. She said that was good. She'd be able to look after me. I grabbed my backpack and left.

I couldn't believe how easy it was.

CHAPTER EIGHTEEN

I went home. I checked the mailbox and picked up
the newspaper at the front door. I reminded myself
that I had to do that every day. I didn't want people
thinking anything had changed around here.

I scrunched up the note I'd left for Andy.

I checked the messages. Nothing.

I checked the kitchen cupboards. Nothing there
either. I was going to get pretty hungry if Andy didn't
show up soon. I had about four dollars left from my
allowance and could probably scrounge up another
two or three dollars in change if I checked all Andy's
pockets, but that was it.

I'd worry about how I was going to survive later.
What I needed to do right then was figure out where
Andy and Byron were. I needed clues.

I ransacked the apartment—the bathroom, the living room, the bedrooms. There was lots there, but nothing that hadn't always been there.

I went through Andy's closet, her drawers, her makeup bag, her laundry, her bedside table, her piles of junk. All I found were old clothes, broken eyeliner pencils and overdue library books.

I went through Byron's stuff. That took, like, four seconds. I guess he wasn't kidding. He wasn't into material things. All he had were the clothes he'd taken off the day before. They were folded neatly on my bed like he'd joined the army or was trying out for a job at the Gap. I poked them with a ruler, flipped them over, shook them. I even stuck my bare hand into the pockets. Nothing.

I kicked the wall for about five minutes, until my foot hurt and the guy downstairs started banging on the floor with his cane. That's all I needed, him calling the cops on me. So I went into the living room and punched the couch for a while. At least it was quiet.

I finally got tired and stopped. For a long time I just lay there, staring at the big stain on the ceiling. It always used to remind me of a bunny in high heels. Sort of cute. But that day I turned my head the other way and realized that the bunny's legs could be somebody's arms, and the high heels could be a couple of guns. That was sort of sick. That's what someone with a disturbed mind would see.

It's bad when you can't trust yourself to stare at the ceiling.

I turned on the TV and sort of watched it until three thirty, when it was safe to go outside. School was out. No one would wonder what I was doing on the street. I grabbed my skateboard and left. I stopped at Toulany's for some snacks. Joe was hunched over the counter, scrolling through his Facebook feed as per usual. He could ring up your order, count your money and make change all without taking his eyes off the screen. The guy was addicted.

I picked up a beef-jerky stick, some sour-cream-and-onion chips and a large cardboard box. I tried to make the food last, but I couldn't. I was starving. I'd inhaled it by the end of the block.

I got to Atula's at about four. Toby gave me a big hug when I walked in, and Marge said she'd sure missed me. Mr. Lucas went on about how much I'd grown, and Elmore Himmelman started screaming that I was an FBI agent who was trying to kill him for his million-dollar inheritance.

That's when Atula came flying out of her office, yelling at people to keep their voices down. Things must have been crazy for her without anyone to help, but she still smiled when she saw me. I told her I was there to collect Andy's stuff, and her smile sort of died. She rearranged that scarf of hers and asked me to stop by her office before I left.

I pried Toby off me, went into Andy's office and shut the door. I started dumping stuff from her drawers into the box. It was mostly loose-leaf pads, message slips, old school pictures of me, that kind of thing. Not what I was looking for. I was looking for evidence—whatever that meant.

I cleaned out the desk, then opened Andy's filing cabinet. That's where I figured all the really good stuff would be.

I was too late.

It was empty.

I had this moment of terror. You know, like in movies when the person who's going to get killed realizes that the phone is dead or the gun is gone. I imagined some thug—Byron, maybe, or whoever he was after—sneaking in with panty hose over his head and rifling through Andy's office. There must have been something incriminating in her files. Something they had to get. Something they were willing to kill for.

Clearly I was getting hysterical. That's not what had happened to the files. Atula had them!

It was obvious. Andy was gone, so Atula was looking after those clients herself now. Who else was going to?

I tried to think of some way I could get the files from her, but I knew that would never happen. There's this thing in law, *solicitor-client privilege*, that means anything you say to your lawyer is private. Even if you tell him you killed somebody or robbed a bank, he's not allowed to say anything about it unless you let him. Same thing with your legal files. They're private. Atula was hardly going to hand them over to me. And I wasn't ready to steal them. At least, not yet. I had to figure this mess out some other way.

I put Andy's daytimer and address book in the cardboard box. I wiped off her desk and threw the dead plant she'd had all summer into the garbage can. I grabbed the box and the coat she'd left hanging on the back of the door and went to see Atula.

Good thing Atula was so busy, because there was no way I could take another lecture or another little "you know I'm here for you" talk. Atula tried to squeeze one in anyway, of course, but the phone rang and she had to get it. While she was talking to the guy, she reached up and rubbed the back of her hand on my cheek. I don't know why, but that made my eyes get all watery. I felt like such a wuss.

I just wanted to get out of there. I was worried I was going to start crying.

Or talking—that would be even worse.

I went, "See ya" and bolted. Toby made a dive for me on the way out, but I was too fast. I said, "Gotta run, Tobe." And I did.

CHAPTER NINETEEN

Real evidence

Evidence supplied by material objects

I got home and dumped the box full of Andy's stuff on the kitchen table. It was pretty depressing. What a pile of useless junk.

I had to organize it somehow, make some sense of it.

I started by throwing out all the garbage, the empty cigarette packs, the wads of gum wrapped up in little bits of tinfoil, the paper clips Andy had bent into weird shapes, but then I changed my mind. I took them all out of the garbage can and put them back on the table. I realized this stuff could be important. Maybe Andy hadn't chewed that gum at all. Maybe somebody else had, and his slimy DNA was all over it. Maybe all I needed was a little bit of his saliva, and the guy would be behind bars for the rest of his life.

I studied every single thing I took from Andy's office, one at a time. This is what I found.

Nothing.

So then I tried to put the stuff in groups. Maybe I'd start seeing a pattern. I put all the "garbage" over on one corner of the table. I put all the pink message slips on another. I put all the photographs together, all the pencils together, and made two piles out of the loose-leaf, used and unused.

Lot of good that did. Sherlock might have been able to see some pattern, but I couldn't.

I read each of the phone messages over again. Darlene, Elmore, Marge. Immigration Resource Center meetings. Appointments with the Crown prosecutor. Reminders for Atula's secretary (yeah right) to call Mr. Bigshot's secretary to confirm the date of the hearing. I was the one who had taken most of the messages, so there were no surprises there. When I went back to school, Andy and Atula just answered the phone themselves or let the machine pick it up. The pink message slips kind of dried up after that.

I looked at the photos. I arranged my school pictures by age, and it suddenly hit me. It was so obvious! Why hadn't I seen it before?

My teeth were way too big for my face! It looked like someone had rammed a couple of Fig Newtons under my top lip. (I guess it would have helped if I'd brushed them.) I made a mental note to get them filed down to normal human size when I had the time.

I looked at the other photos. There was Andy at her graduation. There was Andy at the Poverty Coalition protest. There was Andy outside the new Immigration Resource Center. That one must have been taken the day it opened. Andy and Atula were standing on either side of this giant guy in a business suit. He had his arms around them, and they were all smiling away like a bunch of monkeys who'd just won a lifetime supply of bananas. I figured he was the center's honorary chairman, the guy Andy had gone on and on about. I could even see the fender of his famous green BMW poking out at the bottom of the picture. I thought it was kind of gross, to tell you the truth. Driving up to a place for poor people in a car that cost a hundred thousand bucks. Did nobody else have a problem with that?

Why wouldn't Andy have had a problem with that?

It was stupid to waste my time thinking about that kind of stuff right then. I was supposed to be trying to find Andy, not figure her out. She'd die of old age before I could do that.

I moved on to the next pile, the used loose-leaf. The only thing I learned from it was that my mother is an excellent doodler. I just hoped they had a good art program at the women's penitentiary.

That left the unused loose-leaf. A less sophisticated detective would have just tossed it in the garbage, but that's because a less sophisticated detective wouldn't have spent his childhood years watching *Bobby Smye, Private Eye*. I took a blue crayon and rubbed it over the blank paper. I started to see the imprint of words Andy had written on the missing top sheet. A white phone number appeared in the cornflower blue, and then an address. My heart started to pound. I did another swipe with the crayon, and suddenly I knew what Andy'd been up to. She'd been trying to enroll me in an after-school course! Political Activism for Teens. For a second there, I was almost glad she had disappeared. I wished she'd just stop trying to improve me.

By this time I was mad and frustrated and ready to quit, but if I quit, what would I do then? There was nothing to eat. I couldn't sleep. And I'd kill myself if I tried skateboarding in the shape I was in. I picked up Andy's appointment book and started flipping through it.

It was a mess too, with lots of stuff crossed out or unreadable. Even the stuff I could read looked like it was written in code. *EH Lw. Ct. D&F sep ag? JHG–Hng.*

I'd like to say the Undisputed King of Scrabble had this all figured out in three minutes, but it didn't happen that way. I just stared at the letters for a long time and thought about Kool-Aid Blizzards and Mary MacIsaac and what the chances were that she'd go to the school dance with me if I ever got the nerve to ask her. I came up with a few good lines to make her laugh and started thinking it might not be completely hopeless. Then I realized that the dance wasn't for three more weeks, and if I didn't find Andy by then (or at least some food money), I'd be so scrawny nobody would dance with me. They'd all just lean against the back wall and watch my bones rattle.

I had to concentrate. I looked at the address book again and a couple of things suddenly seemed pretty obvious. *Lw. Ct.* was law court. The capital letters were people's initials. Once I got that, I could pretty much figure out who most people were.

EH. Elmore Himmelman.

D&F. Who else? Darlene and Freddie. So that would mean that *sep ag* was "separation agreement," and the question mark meant "Are they finally going to break up or what?"

JHG–hng. For a second I thought it was "John Hugh Gillis–hanging," but they haven't hanged a man in Canada for, like, forty years. And even then

I doubt they ever hanged someone for a couple of break-and-enters. I guessed that *hng* had to mean "hearing," the one the court set up to figure out what John Hugh's sentence would be on that last B-and-E.

Breaking the code after that was pretty easy. I got stuck on a few words until I realized Andy wasn't just keeping track of work stuff. *TM* was her hairdresser, Taryl Melanson, the one who talked her out of the purple spikes, and *ct* this time wasn't "court." It was either "cut" or, more likely, "chat." (The two of them could gab like you wouldn't believe.) *CM–dnt. ck-up* meant I had an appointment at the dentist that week (I just pretended I didn't understand that one).

But there was one entry showing up over and over again that I couldn't get: *BC–Wtrfrnt.* Andy usually just left out the vowels in the words, so the last part was pretty easy to figure out. *Wtrfrnt* = waterfront. I guessed she'd been meeting somebody at one of those fancy restaurants overlooking the harbor.

Boy, did that make me mad. I'm eating Mr. Noodles for lunch every day while she's out dining like a queen? Aren't mothers supposed to look after their children first?

Even while I was mad, though, I knew something was wrong with this picture. I just couldn't see it—Andy eating out and not even bringing me back a doggie bag. Maybe this wasn't about work either. Maybe this was a boyfriend. I knew she'd had a few over the years, but not because she ever admitted it to me, that's for sure. I'd catch some guy putting his arm around her, or some girlfriend of hers would let slip about Andy's "big date," and Andy would never talk to her again. If she was out having some romantic meal with some new love (barf), she wouldn't bring me back a doggie bag because she wouldn't want me to know about it.

Made sense.

But who was the guy this time?

B.C.

B…C…

B…

C…

I knew someone with those initials. I was sure of it. I ran through all the guys' names I could think of that started with *B*.

Bill. Blair. Brendan. Ben. Bert. Bart.

Byron.

Byron Cuvelier.

B.C.

CHAPTER TWENTY

Minor

A person who is under the age of legal competence.
A child.

I hadn't slept in, like, thirty-six hours. I was so wired I didn't think I'd ever sleep again, but that night I did. I just kind of passed out at the kitchen table. Maybe that's why I had such a weird dream.

Byron was my father, and I had a stump for my hand too, and we were living in this sort of tent thing that we had to keep moving all the time. Kendall lived with us too, I think, or he was around anyway. He gave me this special skateboard that only had three wheels. I could do these amazing moves on it, but only because I was missing a hand. Andy was in the dream too, sort of. You know what dreams are like. I could hear her voice or smell her smoke or talk to her on the phone, but I could never actually see her. One time I even had to wait outside the bathroom while she used it (our tent had a phone and bathroom—quite the camping experience), but somehow she slipped out without my noticing.

The whole dream was like that. I wanted to see her—I'd go looking for her, I'd run after the sound of her voice—but I didn't want to see her too. I knew she'd take away the skateboard, but that wasn't what I was really afraid of.

I was scared she was going to be mad at me when she found out Byron was my father.

As if it was my fault.

It sounds completely stupid now, but when I was dreaming, it was like it was really happening. I was freaked when I woke up. I could barely catch my breath.

I looked around the kitchen for a long time, just telling myself it wasn't real. That helped for a while, until I realized that reality was even worse than any dumb thing I could dream up.

I thought about Byron and Andy having their little secret meetings at the waterfront. What were they thinking? Like they wouldn't stick out there! Andy, in her Salvation Army specials, and the aging chick magnet trying to blend in with all those people in expensive business suits. If they wanted to keep their secret, why would they meet there?

Because they were so in love they couldn't think clearly.

Oh, bleh.

Kek.

Ack. Ack. Ack.

Gag.

I practically barfed. It sort of made sense. I knew Andy acted like she hated Byron and wanted to get rid of him, but you know how weird people can be when they like someone.

I couldn't shake the idea that Byron was Andy's boyfriend and all those late-night arguments were just lovers' spats. It was so gross and probably pretty stupid, but my mind wouldn't give it up. It was like my subconscious or whatever you call it wanted to prove the worst was true, rub my nose in it. It said things to me like *She was just playing hard to get* and *There was obviously something going on. She let him stay, after all!* Somehow blackmail didn't seem like enough of a reason for anyone to put up with Byron.

I saw little pictures of things that had happened while Byron was living with us. Him singing, him giving Andy that "hey, baby" smile, her making sure he got his salad just the way he liked it. Then I remembered seeing that C.C. tattoo on his biceps when we were arm-wrestling, and all the blood ran out of my face. I suddenly knew what it stood for.

Cyril Cuvelier.

I really *was* his son! And the stupid mistake Andy said she'd made when she was a kid was me! And the reason Byron went to jail was because Andy was only fourteen when he got her pregnant, and that's illegal.

Oh, God.

It all fit. I even remembered what they called it. *Statutory rape*—sexual relations with a minor child. An adult can't do it with a kid under sixteen, even if the kid wants to. It was one of the few things they talked about at law school that I actually found interesting.

I wanted to go back to sleep and just forget about everything. But I couldn't. I still didn't know why Andy'd just disappear like this. I still didn't know where she was or what she was doing. I still didn't know how I was going to survive.

I heard the newspaper land at the door. I needed to pee anyway, so I went and got it. I was really stiff, and my eyes burned when I opened the door and the light shone in. I grabbed the paper, slammed the door and went to the can.

I didn't trust my aim, so I sat. I scratched my head and rubbed my eyes. I put my elbows on my knees and looked down at the newspaper on the floor.

There was a big red headline. *Suspect Sought in Masons' Hall Fire.* Below it was a picture, one of those police photographs where the guy holds up a card with numbers on it. The guy was twentysomething, I'd say. He had a mustache that hung below his chin, and one eye was swollen shut, but I still knew right away that it was Byron Cuvelier.

CHAPTER TWENTY-ONE

Arson

The intentional setting of fire to a building

Halifax Daily

SUSPECT SOUGHT IN MASONS' HALL FIRE

ANNA VON MALTZAHN
CRIME BUREAU

Halifax Police have released the name of a suspect wanted in relation to the fire that destroyed a historic landmark and killed a homeless man on August 20 of this year.

Byron Clyde Cuvelier, 37, of no fixed address, is described as being 5'11" and having a slim build and brown eyes. His arms and chest are extensively covered with tattoos and he is missing his right hand. He was last seen at the Life's Work Shelter for Men on the night of the fire. According to witnesses, he left around midnight to go to the Masons' Hall.

Mr. Cuvelier served six years in Dorchester Penitentiary for the robbery that cost him his hand, but is not believed to be dangerous. According to acquaintances, Mr. Cuvelier began frequenting the men's shelter about eight months ago upon his return to Halifax after several years of travel. He was apparently well liked by all.

Gisele Theriault, director of Life's Work, described him as "kind and extremely intelligent. Byron was always helping the other guys with their problems. He spent time in Guatemala doing aid work, so he knows how to relate to people in crisis." Based on his experience, Ms. Theriault had just offered him a part-time job as a counselor at the shelter.

Police are releasing few details, but sources reveal that an anonymous phone call this week provided the first real lead in the suspicious fire that killed Karl Stafford Boudreau, 49.

The Masons' Hall had been vacant for over three years while heritage activists struggled to raise money for its restoration. During that time, homeless men often camped out in the five-story Victorian building. An illegal drug-making operation is believed to be the cause of the fire. Sources say a worker on a construction project next door provided evidence linking Mr. Cuvelier to a crack cocaine operation.

Mr. Boudreau suffered from mental illness and diabetes. Friends say Mr. Cuvelier was often seen helping him with a weight-loss program.

Halifax Police ask that anyone with information regarding the Masons' Hall fire or the whereabouts of Byron Clyde Cuvelier please contact Sergeant Hannah Gautreau at 431-TIPS.

CHAPTER TWENTY-TWO

Conspiracy
The agreement of two or more people to perform an illegal act

That woke me up fast. I ran into the living room and turned on *The Breakfast Show*. I had to sit through about ten minutes of this irritating guy making jokes about the weather, but it finally came on. *Masons' Hall Fire Breakthrough!*

The reporter did a big thing about how the hall had welcomed home our troops from both world wars, and then another thing about all the famous people who'd had their wedding receptions there. I was absolutely screaming at the TV by the time she got to the part about the hall's sad years of decline and how more than once it had been saved from the wrecker's ball by heritage activists who had fought against a new condo development or shopping mall.

I was just about to try another channel when the reporter finally got to the part about the fire and Byron Clyde Cuvelier. That old picture of him flashed on the screen, and then she interviewed a bunch of his buddies at the men's shelter.

You'd swear they were talking about some guy who'd just won the Nobel Peace Prize. Byron Cuvelier could do no wrong as far as they were concerned. One old grandpa with about three teeth in his head and a bad eye said Byron was teaching him to read. Somebody else said Byron helped him give up smoking. A kid who looked about two years older than me said Byron gave him money when his eight-year-old needed a new snowsuit.

Then this guy named Stan Berrigan started ranting away about how the whole thing was a conspiracy. "Byron ain't done nothing wrong. Just 'cause he made a mistake a few years ago and done time, the police is pinning it on him. They always takes it out on the homeless. Like, just because you don't have a roof over your head means you ain't as good as the rich folks. Byron knows that ain't true. He knows a few other things too. I'll bet he knows a few other things that some of them rich folks wouldn't like him spreading round neither."

You could tell the guy wasn't half finished, but the reporter wrapped it up anyway. "And now back to you, Josh, and today's sports!"

Somehow I didn't feel like hearing about the Leafs' season opener. I turned off the TV and stared at that stain on the ceiling again.

Okay, I thought, so this is what happened. Byron Cuvelier, counselor to the homeless by day, was cooking up crystal meth by night. In his drugged-out state, he set a historic building on fire and killed a man.

That at least explained the big blister on his arm.

I'd never liked the guy, so I really wanted to believe my theory was true. But I couldn't.

It just didn't sound like Byron to me.

CHAPTER TWENTY-THREE

Hearsay
Evidence that is heard secondhand

I got a bag of Nacho Krispies at Toulany's and headed off to the shelter to find Stan Berrigan. The whole way there, I thought of all the things I could have believed about Byron. I could have believed he conned an old lady out of her last tube of denture cream. I could have believed he was a terrorist spy for the Home and School Association. Under certain circumstances, I could probably even have believed he was first runner-up in the Miss Nude Universe Pageant.

But I couldn't believe he was a crack dealer, an arsonist and a killer. Even if the fire and the death were accidents, I still couldn't believe Byron was into drugs. The guy couldn't stand cigarette smoke or cheeseburgers. I was supposed to believe he was doing crack?

Okay, maybe he wasn't doing it himself. Maybe he was just selling it. Living the pure life and selling it on the side.

If that's what he was up to, where was the money? What was he doing in a homeless shelter? He just liked the rooms better than at the Westin Hotel?

And how come he was mooching off us? It sure wasn't for the food. He never stopped complaining about it.

The guy didn't have any money—I was pretty sure of it.

So what was Byron really up to?

I got to the men's shelter by about eight in the morning, but I was too late. The guys all get kicked out of bed at seven and aren't allowed back in until nighttime. The lady sweeping up was nice though. She knew Stan Berrigan and exactly where to find him. She sent me downtown to Argyle Street, where all the bars and taverns are. He liked to get there early to collect cigarette butts from the night before.

I found Stan harvesting butts from the sidewalk in front of the Liquor Dome. He didn't look too pleased to be interrupted, but when he realized I wasn't horning in on his territory, he lightened up a bit. I told him I was writing an article for the school newspaper on the Masons' Hall fire and that I'd like to talk to him about Byron. Stan lit a butt, squinted at me like he'd have to think about it, then launched into exactly the same rant I'd heard on TV. I scribbled it all down, just to keep him happy. When Stan finally came up for air, I managed to get in one of my own questions.

"So how long have you known Byron?"

"Oh, Lordy, now there's a tough one. Maybe twenty, twenty-five years. We're from the same town, eh? Both come up to the big city to find our fortunes. Funny, but I didn't manage to find mine. I guess it weren't in the dishwater at the Seahorse Tavern after all."

He elbowed me in the side. I realized I was supposed to laugh, and he carried on.

"Byron, though, was a different story. He done good for a while there. Went to the university and everything. Scholarship boy. His mum was some proud of him. Until everything up and happened, that is."

"What up and happened?" I asked.

"Oh, Lordy, you don't want to get into that. It was awful messy...aw-ful messy. There was some girl—what did he call her?—Squirt or something. Just a little thing, but with a baby of her own already. She was no good, that one. And what a tongue she had on her too. She coulda stripped paint with it. Probably did. And you know what? This is the truth. Byron might have took the fall for it, but it was her what robbed the church."

My mouth was suddenly so dry that my teeth were sticking to my lips. I swished some spit around and managed to croak out another question.

"Wh-why did she rob a church?"

"Oh, you're taxin' me now, boy. This was a long time ago. How do you 'spect me to remember this stuff?"

He took off his tuque and started scratching away at his head with those big cracked hands of his. He was really going at it. Skin and hair and, I don't know, probably little animals too, were flying all over the place. He finally put his tuque back on and relit the butt he'd just stubbed out. He took a drag and then looked at me as if it all had just come back to him.

"This is what I think happened, but you better not write it down. I don't want to get sued or nothing 'cause I got my facts wrong in the newspaper. That a deal?"

"Yeah, deal."

"Okay, then. Here goes. Byron was helping out at the Salvation Army while he was at the university. I guess he was fixing on being a social worker or somethin'. That's how I run into him again too. By that time my wife had took off on me, and I was turning up at the Army shelter every so often. Them days, I had a bad habit of drinking my paycheck away. Anyways, he was working with them 'wayward girls' there—you know, the ones that went and got themselves pregnant—and he met Squishy or whatever damn thing he used to call her. I think he liked her. I mean just *liked* her. Nothin' more. He was a lot older than her, and you know she had that baby too. What man in his right mind would want to take on somebody else's kid, 'specially one that squalled away like that one did?

"Anyways, she was a smart girl once you got past the dirty mouth, and I thinks he thought she could get into the university too. Thing is, she misinterpreted his intentions is my guess. Thought she caught herself a college boy to look after her and that scrawny baby. That was some sorry-looking youngster—"

"So what about the church?"

Stan quit shaking his head over what a pathetic baby I'd been and got back on track.

"Like I says, you can't quote me on this. It was a long time ago, and anyways, what do I knows about women? I only managed to hang on to one myself for seven and a half months before she turned tail and ran, and to tell you the truth, we're probably both the happier for it, but my guess is this. Like I says, Squinty misinterpreted Byron's intentions. She thought it was love. He thought it was charity. When she realized that's what he was thinking, she done what every self-respecting woman does. She got mad—and then she got crazy. She dumped the baby outside Byron's door and took off. Maybe it was for dope or maybe it was just to spite him for not loving her back, I don't know, but she set out to rob that church…what's it called? The one all them rich south-enders go to? Down Oxford Street…big stone thing…First Methodist, that's it! My grand-mother on my father's side was a Methodist, though she weren't rich, of course.

"Anyways, Byron had helped the church raise all this money for some Mexicans who got shook up by some earthquake, and that Squawker went after it. She made a terrible mess of them fancy stained-glass windows church people like so much. I don't know how, but Byron figured out what she was up to and came after her. He cut his hand something awful on the glass, strugglin' with her. I guess he couldn't get her to give back that strongbox no matter what he did. Church people, eh? What were they thinking?

Just leaving the money there until Monday when the bank opened. Don't they know there's sinners out there?

"Anyways, the alarm went off, or someone out walking their dog saw all them broke windows, I don't know, but the police got called and the two of them ran. Three of them, that is. Byron had the baby with him too, if you can believe that.

"It took about a week for the cops to catch 'em, and by that time Byron's hand was so swolled up and full of pus they had to cut her off. I bet they wanted to cut off more than that too. Them church people were madder than hell. They figured Byron had raised all that money just so he could go and steal it and then run off with some teenager and her baby. As far as the good people of Halifax was concerned, he was the lowest of the low, and he never told them no different. And you can bet that little Squishy didn't neither. She may not a got him to marry her, but she got the next best thing. She got to make him pay.

"Near everybody thought the judge was right to throw the book at Byron, but me and the boys down to the shelter had other ideas. We figured he kept his mouth shut 'cause he knew how much Squishy loved that baby of hers. He knew they couldn't charge her with much because she was only fifteen or sixteen, but he also knew they could take the baby away. If that judge found out this was all Squirt's doing, he wouldn't be giving her back no baby to raise. So Byron just went along with his being the bad influence what led the poor girl astray. He got time, and she got off scot-free. That's the truth, and I can see you don't like it no better than I do. Maybe you should sit down, boy."

"No, no. I'm okay. What happened to the girl?"

"Don't know. I heard she changed her name, and I bet right now she's living a respectable life out in the suburbs somewhere. Probably married herself some nice tradesman who don't have the first clue about what she used to get herself up to. But Byron? He loses his hand. He wastes six years of his life in Dorchester Pen. And now they're after him again for somethin' I knows he wouldn't do. I'll tell you somethin', son. In life, things never add up right. They just don't."

CHAPTER TWENTY-FOUR

Restitution
*Repayment for something that has been
lost or stolen*

Stan Berrigan was wrong. This time, things did add
up right. His story all made sense. Andy had calmed
down as she got older, I guess, but not so much that
I couldn't see her doing something demented like
robbing a church.

I could also see why she didn't want me to find
out about it. Throwing herself at a guy. Abandoning
me. Stealing money from earthquake victims.
Letting somebody else take the blame for it. Andy'd
die of shame if I found out about even one of
those things.

No wonder she wasn't very happy when Byron
showed up at our door. She was afraid he was going
to talk, but what could she do? She could hardly turn
him away after what he'd done for us.

Byron added up too. He'd done that hick routine, but I'd never really fallen for it. I always knew he was smarter than that. Way smarter. Only a true genius could figure out how to be that obnoxious.

I could even understand why he'd be like that. Byron had every right to hate us. Andy had an apartment and a law degree and, for a while there anyway, a career. What did Byron get out of being the good guy? A criminal record and half as many fingernails to clip as the rest of us.

I'd be PO'ed too.

For a second there, I thought maybe that's why he'd shown up. Just to make Andy uncomfortable. Just to make her squirm.

But I knew there was more to it than that. Byron had said he needed her for something. My guess, it was something to do with Consuela and the Masons' Hall fire—but what? What did they have in common?

I got back to the apartment by about ten in the morning and picked up the mail. Phone bill. Power bill. Water bill. Something about Andy's student loan. The only good news was another package from War Amps.

I almost laughed when I saw it. Andy and her stupid keys. Then it hit me why she'd been such a big supporter of War Amps all these years. It wasn't just to get her keys back. It wasn't just to help child amputees. It was to keep her honest. Every single day, that little tag on her key chain made Andy think of Byron and what he'd done. She might have treated him like dog dirt, but she knew she still owed him— big-time. In fact, I figured she could spend the whole rest of her life going to anti-poverty protests and keeping crazy people out of jail and making sure no one ever got ripped off on their welfare check again and she'd probably still owe him.

Believe me, if I went to jail and lost my hand as a *favor* (!) to someone else, I'd be looking for a major payback.

I went into the kitchen and tried to get organized again. I dumped all Andy's work garbage back in the cardboard box except for her daytimer, the messages and the photos. I put those on the table. I tore out the front page of the newspaper with the Masons' Hall story on it and put it on the table too. I got out the spy-recorder tape and my notes from Stan. Then I tried to think how all this fit together.

What it all added up to was this: I was dead meat.

I couldn't call the cops, and I couldn't figure it out myself. I was broke. I was alone. My mother had run off without even leaving me anything to eat, unless, of course, you counted her powdered coffee whitener.

So much for "There's dinner in the freezer, sweetie!" What was she trying to do? Rub it in? "You're starving and there's no food! Ha-ha! See ya!"

Hey, I thought, what *was* she trying to do? So much had happened since I got that weird message that I'd never even thought of looking in the freezer. Maybe she knew she had to go, and she really did leave me some food. You could say a lot of stuff about Andy, but you'd have to admit, she always looked out for me.

I yanked open the freezer door, and a puff of cold air rolled out. I was hoping for a frozen lasagna or even a couple of Pizza Pockets, but no such luck. The freezer was empty.

Empty except for a large legal folder.

CHAPTER TWENTY-FIVE

Title

The right to ownership of property

Andy had also said she'd left me money for a treat in the Player's tobacco tin. When I realized dinner was going to be a pile of legal documents, I figured the best treat I could hope for was an overdue electric bill, but I got the tin down anyway.

Eighty-seven dollars in cold, hard cash. Andy must have cleaned out her bank account before she left. That or I'd just found her stash.

I didn't take another look at the folder until I'd gone to Toulany's and bought myself three Swanson Hungry-Man dinners, two liters of chocolate milk, a jumbo bag of Hickory Stix and some Oreos. Joe asked if I was having a party. No, I said, just my lunch. Joe actually stopped scrolling through Facebook long enough to look at me and laugh.

While I was zapping the first dinner, I looked at the folder. Mostly it was just notes Andy had scrawled on loose-leaf. They were a mess. I couldn't decipher them on an empty stomach. I put them aside.

The rest seemed to be real-estate stuff. It looked like Andy had done a title search on the Masons' Hall. A title search is just, like, a particularly boring history of the property. When a building is sold, you have to make sure there hasn't been any funny business and the seller actually owns what he says he owns. That's why you hire a lawyer to check out all the documents showing every time the place changed hands.

And I mean *every time*. The title search we did in law school went all the way back to 1700-and-something when this soldier got a land grant from the king. (The only problem with that one was, the king couldn't prove how he got the land from the Indigenous people, but that didn't seem to bother anyone in those days.)

The Masons' Hall title search didn't go back that far. The Uniacke family bought the property in 1802, and then the Masons bought it in 1886, built the hall in 1888 and sold it to the Heritage Preservation Association of Nova Scotia in 1998.

That was all straightforward enough. The only thing unusual was that an estoppel had been put on the property in 1889. Andy had highlighted the word *estoppel* in yellow and put a big star and a bunch of exclamation marks beside it. Underneath she'd written, *FLLW THE $!*

The estoppel had clearly gotten her dander up, but why?

FLLW THE $! I figured that was "flow the dollar," but that didn't mean anything to me. Then I realized there were two *l*'s there.

Throw in a couple of *o*'s and you get "follow the dollar."

Duh. "Follow the money!" I'd heard Andy use that plenty of times. It's an old police saying. It just means that if you want to find out who committed a crime, find out who got rich off it. Crime is all about motive.

So Andy thought someone had made a pile of money because of the estoppel. Great. But what was estoppel?

I tried it again.

Es.

Top.

Pel.

Oh geez, I remembered that from law school. What I mean is, I remembered the word *estoppel*. I didn't have the first clue what it actually meant.

I was pretty tired by then, but still. You'd think, given that this was a life-or-death type of thing for Andy, I could've come up with something.

But no. I just sat there scratching my head and looking like a baboon doing double-digit division.

What was the matter with me? I actually slapped myself in the side of the head and said, "Smarten up, jerkface."

I needed to find out what estoppel meant.

Like, right away.

I rifled through Andy's room, hoping I could find her old law dictionary, but no luck. She's so disorganized, I don't know why I even bothered. Gives you some idea how desperate I was, I guess.

I chewed on my hangnail for a while and thought.

I could call Atula and ask her what estoppel meant.

That'd work.

No, it wouldn't. She'd just say, "Why don't you ask your mother, Cyril? And by the way, where is your mother?"

Good point.

I could go to the city library and google it.

No again. I remembered that the downtown library was closed for renovations, and I didn't know where the other ones were.

I could go to the law library.

Wrong. I needed an identification card to get in there.

Wrong right back at you! I had an identification card! Andy's ID.

I even knew where it was. I could see it from where I was standing. Andy used it to prop open her window so she could smoke in her bedroom and I wouldn't know. (Nice try.)

I yanked it out, and the window slammed shut. I couldn't believe my luck. The ID card was bent and dirty, but it was still good for a couple of months.

There was only one problem.

It was a picture ID. Having Andy's card wouldn't do me any good because I didn't have Andy's face.

CHAPTER TWENTY-SIX

Misrepresentation
Conduct, or a statement, that gives a false
impression

If I'd had more time, I could've come up with a better
solution. I know I could have. I mean, even while
I was pulling on Andy's skirt, other schemes were
running through my head. I could call Jeannie
Richardson from Andy's law-school class. I could
track down that Craig guy who had the hots for
her. Geez, any lawyer could have told me what
estoppel meant.

But I couldn't ask. I couldn't waste the time trying
to find them. I couldn't risk anyone getting suspicious. I just had to forget about that. I went back to
rooting around in Andy's drawer until I found some
panty hose that sort of matched. I considered stuffing
a bra with socks and putting that on too, but there
are limits to how far a guy will go to save his mother.

I pulled on the boots with the biggest heels and hoped they made me look tall enough, put about fifteen rings on my fingers and started wrapping my head in bandages. Completely in bandages. I'm talking *Return of the Mummy*. You know, nothing showing but my eyes. If anyone asked, I'd just say I'd had a terrible accident.

No. No.

I'd say, "I had massive plastic surgery."

That cracked me up. Andy would kill me for saying that.

I slapped myself for laughing at a time like this, threw on her coat and left.

Then came back.

Andy's got blue eyes. I've got brown.

Would anyone notice? I was getting paranoid, I guess, but I didn't want to blow my cover over a stupid little thing like that. I pulled the tips of my ears out from under the bandages, hung some sunglasses on them and left again.

Mr. Bradley, the commissionaire, was checking IDs at the law library. Good thing I'd worn the sunglasses. He'd have known right off the bat that Andy's eyes weren't brown. He was about eighty, but still looking for action. Always talking up the babes. Can you believe these old guys? I guess they figure if you're decrepit enough you can get away with anything.

Still, I've got to give him credit. He practically started to cry when he realized, or when he thought he realized, it was Andy under all those bandages. "Oh, my land! What *happened* to you, girlie?"

"Nothing," I scribbled in his logbook. "Just a little plastic surgery."

"Plas-tic *surgery*! What'd you go do a thing like that for?" He looked at me like I'd just sawed my own legs off. "You had such a gorgeous kisser already!" I waved my hand like, *Aw, shucks* and wrote that I'd be all better next week and more beautiful than ever. Wink. Wink. Nudge. Nudge.

He shook his head and said, "You come back then and let old Gus decide about that. "

I nodded. He let me in.

I went straight to the law dictionaries. Nobody even took a second look at me. They were all too polite.

I found the *E*'s and flipped to the page I needed. Lawyers seem to use the word *estoppel* like the rest of us use *thingamajig*. I scanned through a bunch of definitions.

ESTOPPEL BY DEED.
ESTOPPEL BY RECORD.
PROMISSORY ESTOPPEL.

No.

No.

No.

ESTOPPEL BY CONDUCT.

Hmm.

When one person leads another to believe that certain facts are true, and these are acted upon, then in subsequent proceedings this person cannot deny the truth of such facts.

It was all coming back to me now. It wasn't even as complicated as it sounded. (Sometimes you gotta wonder if lawyers don't just make stuff seem confusing so people will have to pay them to explain it.)

There was this case I remembered drilling Andy on for her property exam. It went something like this. Mr. A. built a house. Part of it was on his neighbor's land. Let's call her Ms. B. Ms. B. knew the house was on her property but didn't try to do anything about it until after the house was built. Then she took Mr. A. to court to have the house moved. The judge didn't go for it. She said, "You knew Mr. A. was building the house on your land. You should have said something before he finished it. It costs way too much to expect him to move it now."

See, it's all about equity. (That's one of those I'm-smarter-than-you legal words. It just means "fairness.") It wouldn't be fair to make the poor sucker tear his house down. But it wouldn't be fair to just give the neighbor's land to him either.

That's why the judge applied the "principle of equity" to the case. She, like, fiddled with the law until it was fair.

The judge put an "estoppel" on the property. That meant Mr. A. didn't have to move the house, but if anything ever happened to it—say, it burned down, for instance—Ms. B. would get her land back to use any way she wanted.

I slammed the dictionary shut and tried to say, "Bingo!" That was why Andy had highlighted the word *estoppel*. She was thinking somebody had benefited from torching the Masons' Hall. Somebody who wanted the land back. But who?

And how was Byron connected?

I chewed on that question all the way home on the bus. I could almost hear the *Jeopardy!* theme music playing.

Da-di da da. Da-di-dahhh. Da-di da da. Da-di…

Just before the buzzer sounded, I answered. "Ahhh…who are homeless people, Alex?"

The newspaper article said homeless people like Byron and that friend of his who died used to sneak into the empty Masons' Hall and hang out.

Maybe Byron had seen something there he wasn't supposed to.

Or maybe someone had talked Byron into burning the place down for them. Told him it was for the good of humanity.

Or maybe Byron was taking the rap for someone else, though you'd think he would have learned to quit taking the rap by now.

They all made sense, sort of.

I got off the bus, picked up my skirt and booted it the rest of the way home. People looked at me strangely. This one guy grabbed my arm and said, "Should you be running in your condition? Can I help you?" I shook his hand off and kept running. I had to. I'd just remembered I'd left my turkey dinner in the microwave.

CHAPTER TWENTY-SEVEN

Suspect

A person wanted by the law in relation to a crime

The turkey was looking pretty sad by the time I got there, but I didn't care. It was two thirty. I was starving. I ripped off just enough bandages to get a fork in and started hoovering my way through my cold and crunchy Hungry-Man dinner.

I gorged for a while. It was great. It was like being a little kid again. The only thoughts going through my head were, Mmmmm. Yummy. Yummmy. Yeah…yeah. Mmmmm. More, more, more, more, more, more, more!

That didn't last. Once my hunger got under control, my brain kicked back in. I started to think about all the stuff I was getting hit with. It was a lot to digest—the stuff, I mean, not the dinner. (Frankly, they never put in enough mashed potatoes for me.)

I was just mulling it all over and sort of absent-mindedly fiddling with stuff on the table when I flipped over that picture of Andy at the Immigration Resource Center. There was something written on the back that I hadn't noticed before.

Left to right: Atula Varma–Varma and Associates Law Office; Bob Chisling–Honorary Chairman, Immigration Resource Center, and President, Waterfront Construction Ltd.; Andi McIntyre–Varma and Associates.

Hmph, I thought, they spelled Andy's name wrong. I bet she was wild about that. I was just picking the peas out of the gravy (I was hungry, but not hungry enough to eat peas) when something else hit me about the caption. I picked up the photograph again. *Waterfront.* Kind of a coincidence, I thought, Andy spending so much time at the waterfront and this guy being president of Waterfront Construction.

Then I thought, Bob Chisling.

B.C.

BC–Wtrfrnt

I dropped my fork, grabbed Andy's daytimer and started flipping through it. I checked the times Andy had met with B.C.

Three forty-five PM.

Four PM.

Five fifteen PM.

If she'd been meeting with Byron, I would have known about it. I would've been home—and Byron wouldn't have been.

B.C. couldn't have been Byron.

That was a relief, but it was sort of a drag too. Andy meeting with Byron down at the waterfront was the only real "fact" I'd had up till then. Everything else was just me making up theories, based on other theories, based on other theories, based on other theories…

It kind of made me feel like giving up again, but I didn't. I just kicked the table, flicked a few peas at the window and got on with it. I said to myself, Okay. What if B.C. is Bob Chisling? Where does that get me?

I turned to the day Andy went missing. She was supposed to meet B.C. at three o'clock that day. Maybe she had, or maybe he was the important colleague Atula said Andy had left hanging. Bob Chisling, president. It fit.

Then I thought about FLLW THE $. I remembered that big fancy BMW of his. The guy clearly liked money. I looked at the photo again. The caption said B.C. ran a construction company.

Just where was he constructing stuff? Anywhere near the Masons' Hall, by any chance?

Time for an Internet search. I couldn't face flirting with Mr. Bradley at the law library again. There had to be somewhere I could get on the Internet around here without having to go there in drag.

Toulany's.

Joe was always online, and I figured he owed me. A third of the money in that Player's tobacco tin had ended up at his store.

I tore off Andy's clothes and threw my own back on. My apartment key was somewhere under the junk on the kitchen table. I was in no mood to start looking for it. I just tore open the War Amps envelope and left with Andy's keys.

CHAPTER TWENTY-EIGHT

Zoning bylaws
Rules made for the regulation, administration or management of a certain district

You'd swear I'd asked Joe to give me one of his kidneys. He looked up from his laptop and said, "Get your own."

I said, "C'mon, Joe. You know Andy! What're the chances she's going to pay for Wi-Fi? Zero. I got a geography project due tomorrow. You don't want me to fail, do you?"

He looked up and glared at me.

"Ten minutes," he said. "And don't be checking my browser history either." He pushed the laptop at me.

"You're a prince, Joe."

He swatted me away with his hand and said, "Sit over there where people can't see you. I don't want anyone getting the idea they can just come in here and use my laptop like this is some goldarn Internet café or something."

I put it on the chest freezer in the corner and got busy.

Bob Chisling wasn't shy, that was for sure. When I punched his name into Google I got about three hundred references. He was on every charity organization that would have him. He particularly loved diseases. Cancer, MS, irritable bowel syndrome... after a while it got so I wouldn't have been surprised to see him raising money for the Acne Breakout Prevention Society or the Chronic Jock Itch All-Star Scratch-a-Thon.

On August 20—believe it or not—when he could have been in dear old Halifax enjoying the gala birthday celebrations of Cyril F. MacIntyre, Chisling was in Moose Jaw, Saskatchewan. There was a picture of him coming first in a celebrity bike race in support of, get this, halitosis research. (Halitosis. In other words, bad breath. Like that needed research. Had these guys never heard of Tic Tacs?)

Chisling was also big into immigration stuff, but I already knew that. There was an article in the *Street People Daily* that talked about all the money he gave to the new Immigration Resource Center and all the immigrants he'd helped over the years. He had this big sob story about how his mother was a Cuban refugee who came here after the revolution, so he knew how hard starting life in a new country could be.

At first glance, I had to admit Bob Chisling didn't look like the kind of criminally inclined individual who'd go and burn a building down.

His business seemed to be perfectly respectable too (like I would know). I got the feeling from the articles that he built mostly apartments and condos, that kind of stuff. Not in my neighborhood though. He built them downtown or on the water. Places rich people like to live. He'd even bought the old Birchy Head Yacht Club way out on St. Margaret's Bay and was trying to turn that into condos. There was this one story all about the big party he threw to celebrate the announcement of "Birchy Head Estates." He sounded just thrilled to pieces.

"St. Margaret's Bay has never seen anything like Birchy Head Estates!" crowed well-known philanthropist and developer Robert (Bob) Chisling. "Premium construction, luxurious surroundings and, of course, its world-class ocean vistas will make this new gated community the most coveted address in Eastern Canada!"

Bob didn't seem so happy in the next article though. A group of people who lived in Birchy Head had taken him to court. Legally, I guess he wasn't allowed to put houses on a property zoned for recreation. He went to court to apply for a change of the zoning, but the locals wouldn't go for it. The judge stopped the construction. There was a big picture of Chisling, looking like none of his friends had bothered to come to his birthday party.

"The legal obstacle we're facing is of course very frustrating for us," said the 43-year-old former bartender who reportedly paid over $3 million for the dramatic seaside property. "But I'm most concerned about its devastating effects on the economy of St. Margaret's Bay. Birchy Head Estates would have brought hundreds of new jobs to this economically disadvantaged area. I just don't know where those people are going to find work if this project doesn't go ahead."

The article that interested me the most, though, was *Waterfront Purchases Haliburton Building.* It was just a little blurb saying:

Bob Chisling, president of Waterfront Construction, announced the purchase of the former Haliburton Building for $2.6 million. Located next door to the historic Masons' Hall, the building will be converted to luxury residential units. Opening is expected in June of next year.

My eyes got big. *Next door to the Masons' Hall.* I wondered if that estoppel could have been interesting to Mr. Chisling. I was pretty sure I was onto something when I opened "City Hall Notes."

Waterfront Construction Project Shut Down. *An application to amend zoning bylaws on the former Haliburton Building was voted down last night. The development does not offer sufficient parking space for a five-story residential project. In response to the closure of this multi-million-dollar development, Robert Chisling, President, Waterfront Construction, said, "The legal obstacle we're facing is of course very frustrating for us…"*

Blah, blah, blah.

The guy clearly needed some new material.

I don't know anything about money. To me, eighty-seven dollars stuffed in a Player's tobacco tin is a fortune. Bob Chisling probably paid more than that for a pair of jockey shorts. But I couldn't help thinking that having two construction projects shut down in under a year must have been pretty expensive, even for him. You buy a property, you've got to pay the mortgage (that's about all I got out of the class in real-estate law). How was he going to pay the mortgage if he couldn't sell the condos? If he couldn't even build them?

I logged off and handed the laptop back to Joe, who'd been panting like a chained dog ever since he'd let me have it.

"Find what you needed?" he grunted as he logged in to Facebook.

"I hope not," I said and headed down to Barrington Street.

There was a big wooden fence up around where the Masons' Hall used to be. This was really sad. It used to be a cool building, with all those curlicues and everything. They sure knew how to make 'em back then.

I turned the corner onto Prince Street. There was a big sign on the building right behind the Masons' Hall property. *Opening next October: Haliburton Place! Another Quality Development from Waterfront Construction Ltd.*

What do you know? It looked like, thanks to that fire, Bob Chisling had suddenly managed to find himself some parking space.

CHAPTER TWENTY-NINE

Trespass

Unlawful interference with another's person, property or rights

I don't know what I thought I was going to see, but I decided to sneak behind the big wooden fence and take a look around. The Haliburton Building was empty, and what used to be the Masons' Hall was just a giant black hole. No one was around—I guess they'd all quit for the day—so I started kicking through the ashes, looking for...I don't know, something suspicious, I guess. Hey, you know me! Cyril MacIntyre, Arson Investigator.

What a joke. Arson is, like, the hardest crime there is to solve, even for the professionals. (Think about it. The evidence literally goes up in smoke.) Did I really believe I was going to break this case? It was like looking for a needle in a humongous barbecue pit.

I was all ready to go anyway when this guy in a hard hat came out of the Haliburton Building and started screaming at me. "Hey, you! Kid! What are you doing here? Can't you read? No trespassing! Now git! Git out of here before I throw you out."

The way he was coming at me, I was pretty sure he meant it. I was just making plans to dive back through the crack in the fence when another voice started drowning the guy out.

"Calm down, Danny! Calm down. He's just a kid." I turned around and saw Bob Chisling smiling at me. I recognized him immediately. He was even bigger than he looked in photographs, and he was all decked out again in a business suit and tie. He was one of those guys who had to look rich all the time. Even in a pile of rubble.

"He's right, though, Bud," he said. "You shouldn't be in here. Construction sites are dangerous."

"Oh, sorry," I went. "I was just, ahhh, interested in seeing what was going on back here."

How true. How true.

Chisling laughed and tossed me his hard hat. "I was just like you when I was a kid! Here! Put this on, and I'll give you a little tour."

Danny, that first guy, rolled his eyes and shook his head so hard I thought his teeth were going to come out. Apparently he didn't agree with encouraging youthful curiosity in the construction trade.

Bob the Builder, though, was a regular award-winning website of information. He showed me the blueprints and how the Haliburton Building was being stripped down to its bare bones—excuse me; lathes, they call them—and rebuilt. He even took me up to the fifth floor so I could look at the harbor from the "premier luxury penthouse suite."

I said, "It's a beautiful view."

He said, "Thanks."

I said, "Especially since the Masons' Hall burned down, I guess."

His eyelid twitched, but otherwise he acted almost normal. He wiped some dirt off that fancy suit of his while he figured out what to say next. He finally came up with, "What a tragedy that was." He shook his head sadly, like this was really breaking him up, then clapped his hands together and said, "Hey, I'm sure glad I got to meet you, but sorry, Bud, I've got to get going now."

I made a big deal about how nice he'd been to show me around. When we got back to the front door he said, "When you're a little older, why don't you look me up? I'll see about getting you a job around here. You seem pretty interested in construction."

"Oh, thank you very much," I said, "but I'm afraid I don't know your name." I sounded so sweet I almost gagged.

"Geez, what was I thinking?" he said. "Bob Chisling."

I was still shaking that big bear paw of his when I said, "Bob Chisling? You're Bob Chisling? I think you know a friend of mine!"

"Oh yeah? Who?"

"Andy MacIntyre."

You know when you get your school picture taken, and they catch you with your eyes half open and your lips all crooked? That's what happened to Bob. His whole face just sort of froze with this weird look on it. It was like he'd been zapped with a stun gun. He finally shook himself out of it. He swallowed and smoothed his perfect hair and looked up at the sky like he was thinking this over really hard. "Andy MacIntyre? An-dy…MacIntyre?" he said. "No. Nope. Sorry, but I don't think I know her."

CHAPTER THIRTY

Mens rea (Latin)
An evil intention, a guilty mind

They say things never turn out as bad as you think they're going to.

I used to believe that, and for most of my life it had been true. There weren't crocodiles under my bed after all. My second-grade teacher didn't tie kids up and stuff them in her desk. Nobody laughed when I got up to dance. And Andy and I never ended up on the street.

Something good always happened.

A check arrived. Andy got a job. Someone gave us their second-slice-is-free pizza coupons. No matter what, life never stank as much as I thought it was going to. In fact, it always kept on getting a tiny bit better than it was before. I remembered when all we had was a mattress on the floor, a table and a chair that smelled like Parmesan cheese. Now we had two mattresses on the floor, two bureaus, a couch, lamps, kitchen chairs and a TV that pretty much always worked. In my heart, I truly believed that if things kept going the way they were, someday we'd probably even have cable too.

Then this happened. Through everything— Byron showing up, Andy disappearing, Atula firing her—a little voice in the back of my head kept saying, "It'll be okay. Something will come through." But it didn't. It just went from bad to worse to really, really horrible.

That's what this was. Really, really horrible.

I was walking home from the Haliburton Building after running into Chisling. It was seven at night, just getting dark, and I was shaking like a rocket right before it lifts off. Or a bomb before it blows. That's how scared I was.

I'd found a motive for burning down the building— parking space. I'd found the guy who had the motive— Bob Chisling. And I knew he knew Andy. I had that picture of them together. I could have believed, maybe, that he didn't remember Andy. A mover and shaker like Big Bob probably met lots of people. But if that was the case, then why didn't he say, "I don't think I know *him*"?

Chisling said, "I don't think I know *her*." If someone mentioned some unknown Andy to you, wouldn't you naturally think they were talking about a guy? I would, and my mother's name is Andy.

Bob Chisling knew her, and I had this sick feeling that he knew where she was too.

My guess was, Andy had followed the money and come to the same person I had. Bob Chisling. Only difference was, she couldn't keep her big mouth shut. She decided to tell him she was onto him.

I didn't know what happened after that, but if I was right and Chisling was the kind of guy who'd burn down a building just to park a few cars, what would he be willing to do to someone who got in his way?

What had he done to her already?

I pictured Bob taking—no, I'm not even going to tell you what I pictured. I don't even like to think about it. It totally freaked me out. My teeth were chattering so hard my eyes were blinking out Morse code messages. I was sure I was going to trip. I didn't want anyone to think there was something the matter with me. With my luck they'd call a doctor— or the police.

I had to sit down. Look normal. (For someone like me, that's a lot harder than it sounds.) There was a big windowsill on the coffee shop. I edged along the wall and parked myself there. I tried to act like I was just waiting for the bus.

I breathed in and out.

In and out.

In...

And out.

I closed my eyes. I just kept taking these long, slow breaths until I stopped shaking. I got kind of woozy from all the oxygen, then kind of dreamy, and then I had this really nice thought. It instantly made me feel all better. I smiled. I couldn't help it. I opened my eyes. I got up and practically skipped the rest of the way home.

This is what I thought: I'm not that smart.

CHAPTER THIRTY-ONE

Sue

*To bring a civil proceeding against a person;
to take someone to court*

Like, who was I kidding? I was thirteen years old.
Did I really think I was smarter than the police? That
I was the only person who knew what an estoppel
was? That the cops wouldn't be onto Chisling too,
if he'd actually done anything?

Clearly, I'd made a mistake. Clearly, Chisling wasn't
guilty. He didn't burn down the building, so he wouldn't
have kidnapped Andy either. He wouldn't have had
any reason to. She was probably just late for dinner
like she'd said she was going to be. Like, *days* late.

Boy, it felt good being stupid. For about ten
minutes, that is.

I was a block or two from home when I remembered the look on Chisling's face. I stopped feeling
good. Innocent people's eyes don't go that psycho.

Chisling was behind the fire, and he was behind Andy's disappearance. I was sure of it. I couldn't pretend he wasn't just to make myself feel better. The estoppel. The parking. The rabid-dog eyes. It all made sense.

So why weren't the police after him? I started kicking a pop can up the street and considered the possibilities.

Maybe they didn't know about the estoppel. It was a hundred years old. Maybe nobody had thought to do a title search.

Could be, I guessed, but you'd think the Heritage Preservation people would know about it. They'd bought the Masons' Hall. They would have done a title search. Somebody would probably mention it to the police. It would be an obvious motive for burning the building down.

Or maybe the cops had so much evidence against Byron that it wasn't worth following any other leads. People knew Byron was going to the Masons' Hall that night. The cops had found his fingerprints there. He had disappeared right after the fire. He was an ex-con. Hey, if I didn't know the guy, I'd think he torched the place too.

But there was another possibility. The one that made most sense to me.

Maybe the cops had put two and two together and gotten the same answer I had. That Chisling set the fire.

All right, then, why weren't the police charging him? I winged the pop can into the side of MacLeod's Drugstore a few times and thought about it. What did I know about the fire?

It was a protected heritage property.

The pop can made this really satisfying *pwong* sound when it hit the aluminum siding.

Homeless people went there.

Pwong.

A guy died.

Pwong.

On August 20.

Pwong.

Pwong.

Pwong.

Hmm, I thought. That was a big day. The Masons' Hall burned down, I became a teenager…but something else had happened too. What was it?

I had this little brain tickle going on. Like I had an itch I couldn't scratch. I was forgetting something important. Something about that day…

I winged the pop can some more and tried to think.

What had happened on my birthday?

Nothing. The usual. Work. A Big Mac combo. A game of Scrabble.

I still had the brain tickle. There was something else.

I wound up and booted the pop can as hard as I could. It banged into the drugstore window and bounced onto the street.

I don't know if it was the way the pharmacist's breath steamed up the window when he yelled at me or the big ad for Listerine on the wall, but suddenly I got it.

Halitosis.

Bike race.

Chisling had won the halitosis bike race on my birthday!

In Saskatchewan.

That was it!

Chisling was a zillion miles away on the day of the fire. He didn't do it. He couldn't have.

You'd think I'd feel good about that, but I didn't. It just meant I was back on the roller coaster again.

He didn't do it. I saw the picture in the paper.

He did do it. I saw the look on his face.

Did not do it.

Did so.

Did not.

Did so.

I went back and forth and back and forth. Chisling did it—he had the motive. Chisling didn't do it—he had an airtight alibi.

At least now I knew why the cops weren't charging him. Even if they thought he had something to do with the fire, they needed proof. Real proof. Evidence. Eyewitnesses. Reasonable and probable cause. Without it, they couldn't do a thing. Charge Chisling on a hunch, and he'd sue the pants off them.

I guess that meant I had an advantage over the police. I didn't need proof. I just needed to find Andy.

CHAPTER THIRTY-TWO

Harboring a fugitive
Hiding a criminal from justice

I let myself back into the apartment with Andy's keys. I wanted to just turn on the TV loud enough that I didn't have to listen to my brain fight with my gut anymore. But I didn't. I sat down, stared at the wall and tried to figure out a theory that made sense. What was everybody up to, and why? It took me a long time to put all the pieces together, but this is what I came up with.

Byron was in the Masons' Hall the night it burned down. He saw something. Maybe he saw somebody start the fire. But he was an ex-con trespassing on private property. Who was going to believe him? Maybe he even guessed the cops would blame it on him.

He already knew about Andy somehow—my guess was through the Immigration Resource Center.

He was a big volunteer, and he spoke Spanish. I could see him helping out down there. Maybe he'd seen her or heard about her and realized that that big-time lawyer (ha-ha) was little Squeaky, all growed up. He didn't say anything—he probably wanted to see her even less than she wanted to see him—but then the fire happened, and he needed her. He needed a place to hide. Byron tracked her down. She took him in.

The thing that stumped me for a long time was Consuela. What did she have to do with it? I went through everything I knew about her.

She was an immigrant.

A Spanish-speaking immigrant. That would be a connection with Byron. Maybe he was one of the few people she could talk to.

She was a Spanish-speaking immigrant with a bandaged arm.

Was that a burn by any chance?

I ran into the kitchen and took another look through the freezer file. It was time to decipher Andy's notes. What did Consuela tell her at that meeting in the park?

I looked at the loose-leaf and realized I might never know. Andy's handwriting was unbelievably bad. I mean, I could have written more clearly with a broken crayon stuck between my toes.

I'd seen notes like this before. Andy used to do the same thing in class—not look at what she was writing and then get home and have no idea what the scrawls meant. I remembered lots of nights trying to help her figure it all out. I guessed I should be glad I'd had such good practice.

I smoothed down the paper. I squinted at it. I turned it upside down. After half an hour this was about all I could make out.

C.R. imm 2 yrs ago. Kds in Mex. Hsekpr 4 BC. In Jn BC accsd CR stlng $$$. BC dprt CR?

See DOH-NUTZ.

BC sd bldg wd b mt & no 1 gt hrt. K died. CR wnt to BC. BC sd jail. Nvr see kds.

CHAPTER THIRTY-THREE

Menaces

Threats of injury in order to force a person to give up something of value

Have you ever had a test you forgot to study for?

That's what this was like.

I stared at the words for a long time, thinking, I have no idea what any of this means. I'm going to fail! But this time, instead of somebody giving me a lecture about how it was my responsibility to know when my homework was due, somebody was going to hurt my mother.

If they hadn't already.

That kind of helped me focus on the problem in front of me.

I got practical. I tried not to think about what I didn't know and started to concentrate on what I did know.

DOH-NUTZ. Easy—and typical. Andy was hungry. Kind of weird, I thought, that she'd have to make a note to herself about it right in the middle of talking to Consuela, but that was Andy. Kind of weird.

One word down, thirty-three to go.

After a while I realized the rest wasn't as hard as I thought it was going to be. Andy was just doing that thing again where she left out the vowels. I could see "kids" and what I figured was "June." Some of the other abbreviations I recognized from Andy's law-school notes. Sd=said. Mt=empty. Imm=immigrant/ immigrate. And *Dprt* had to be "deport."

But the thing that really hit me was *Hsekpr B.C.*

Think about it. Hsekpr. B.C.

Housekeeper. Bob Chisling.

Consuela was Chisling's housekeeper! That's why she was there. That was the connection.

I was so pumped now. I knew exactly how scientists must feel when they discover a cure for cancer, or the dweeb gene, or the way to keep Cocoa Puffs crispy even in milk. It was like, *Yes!* I could do this. I could work this out myself. I went flying through the rest of Andy's notes.

C.R. imm 2 yrs ago. Kds in Mex. Hsekpr 4 BC. In Jn BC accsd CR stlng $$$. BC dprt CR?

Consuela immigrated to Halifax two years ago. Left her kids in Mexico. Worked as a housekeeper for Bob Chisling. In June Chisling accused her of stealing lots of money. Bob said he could have her deported.

I skipped the *See DOH-NUTZ* thing and went on.

BC sd bldg wd b mt & no 1 gt hrt. K died. CR wnt to BC. BC sd jail. Nvr see kds.

Chisling said the building would be empty and no one would get hurt. K died. Consuela went to Chisling. Chisling said jail. Never see your kids.

Consuela knew Chisling had set the fire! She was going to rat on him! He said if she did, he was going to charge her for stealing the money.

Yes! I had it.

No. I didn't.

Chisling was in Saskatchewan on the night of the fire. I kept forgetting that.

I stared at the paper again. All the words made sense now, but they didn't add up right yet. What was I missing?

DOH-NUTZ!

Why hadn't I thought of this before? Andy didn't write *dnts* or *dnuts* or *donuts* or whatever little code word she needed to remember to pick up a dozen on the way home.

She wrote *Doh-nutz*. The name of the chain. In fact, she wrote *DOH-NUTZ* in great big letters. She was talking about a legal case! Suddenly it was all coming together.

You know how Andy used to go crazy when I made fun of Atula's clients. She'd give me those lectures about "how the world really works." She had a homeless lecture. ("All I'd have to do is lose my job, and we could end up on the streets ourselves. So I wouldn't be so smart if I were you, Cyril MacIntyre.") She had a crazy-person lecture. ("One in three Canadians ends up with a mental illness sometime in their life. It could be Atula. It could be me—or it could be you. So I wouldn't be so smart if I were you, Cyril MacIntyre.") And she had a poverty lecture. ("In this country, three hundred thousand kids a month survive on food from the Food Bank. Someday it could be three hundred thousand and one. So I wouldn't be so smart if I were you, Cyril MacIntrye.")

Andy also had an immigrant lecture. That's what came barreling back to me right then. Or, at least, bits and pieces of it did. We'd been on our way to Tony's Donairs for supper one night, and I made some crack about the Korean guy who used to come into Atula's. I can't even remember what it was. Andy went nuts and started ranting away at me about parents who have to leave their kids behind so they can come to Canada and make some money just to survive. About how hard it is to live in a place where you can't speak the language. About how easy it is to be taken advantage of. Blah, blah, blah.

Then she started telling a story about this guy from Afghanistan, I think it was, who got a job working in a Doh-Nutz shop in town here. People would come to the drive-through window and order some type of donut the store didn't sell—say, anchovy fudge crullers or cauliflower Danishes or something like that. The Afghan guy was confused, but what did he know about donuts? The owner told him it was nothing to worry about, to just hand the customers these special Doh-Nutz boxes he kept behind the counter. The Afghan guy was supposed to ring it in as a dozen apple fritters and put the envelope the customer gave him in the cash register.

Anyway, one day the Afghan guy dropped a box by mistake and it popped open, and he saw a little bag of drugs stuffed into one of the donut holes. He was going to tell the police, but the owner found out and said, "Look. You're the guy that's been selling the drugs. Your fingerprints are all over the box. You call the cops, and who are they going to believe? Me, a successful Canadian businessman? Or you, some immigrant just off the boat? Go ahead. Call. See if I care. They'll send you back to rot in some Afghan jail so fast you won't know what hit you." The Afghan guy was too scared to do anything about it. It probably would have gone on like that for years if some new employee hadn't accidentally donated the "Cocaine Crunch" donuts to a church tea and sale. (I wish I'd seen that.)

That's why Andy had written See DOH-NUTZ. That's why in the weird phone message she left me after she disappeared, she told me to buy a box of donuts with "the special filling." She was trying to tell me the same thing had happened to Consuela. Somebody had set her up, then threatened to deport her. I chewed on my hangnails while I reworked my theory.

Okay. I knew Chisling was already in money trouble because both of his construction projects had gotten shut down. He needed to start building again. Let's say he'd somehow found out about the estoppel on the Masons' Hall. He knew that if anything "happened" to the building, the land under it went back to him. He couldn't help thinking it would make a lovely parking lot.

But how was he going to get rid of it? I think Andy thought it was pretty simple. All he had to do was fake the robbery, blame it on Consuela, then blackmail her into burning down the hall for him while he was conveniently out of town.

I knew it sounded a little far-fetched, but maybe that's why Chisling was getting away with it. He couldn't risk burning the building down himself. He also couldn't risk asking around until he found someone he could pay to do it for him. What if they blabbed?

But what was the downside of forcing Consuela to do it? He didn't have to pay her. She was too scared to talk. And if she was like most mothers, she'd do whatever she had to do to see her kids again.

It was perfect—in a sick sort of way.

I decided to ask Consuela if I was right.

CHAPTER THIRTY-FOUR

Ward of court

A minor child under the care of a guardian

There were only two Chislings in the Halifax phone book. One who lived on Artz Street, just around the corner from us (I was willing to bet that wasn't Big Bob), and one on Bloomingdale Terrace.

La-di-dah.

That sounded just like the kind of place he'd live in.

I thought for a second about heading over on my skateboard and knocking on the door, but I couldn't do that. Bob knew my face, and I didn't think he'd be too happy to see it again.

I decided to call Consuela on the phone instead. I know that sounds kind of stupid, because she didn't speak much English and I didn't speak Spanish, but I'd thought of a way around it—I hoped.

I knew a few Spanish words from Bonanza Burrito commercials (and Speedy Gonzales cartoons, of course—who says watching TV is a waste of time?). She knew Byron's and Andy's names. And she had to know where Citadel Hill is. (It's this big giant fort right in the middle of town. Everybody knows where Citadel Hill is.)

So this is what I was going to say (and I was going to say it really, really slowly): "Byron...Andy... Mañana...Citadel Hill...¿Qué hora es? Uno."

I knew *mañana* meant "tomorrow," and I really, really hoped that *¿Que hora es?* meant "What time is it?" and not "How hot do you like your Bonanza Burrito?" *Uno* had to mean "one." What else could it mean?

If everything went right, I'd be meeting her the next day at the Citadel at one o'clock. I figured that would give me enough time to find a good Spanish-English dictionary.

I called the phone number and put on this really cheesy accent. "A-lo. I woulda lika to speaka to Consuela Rodriguez."

A woman who sounded Spanish answered the phone. "I'm sorry, but Consuela ees no long-air hhhere."

I sort of knew she'd say that even before she said it.

"Canna youa tell me wherea she issa?"

"Consuela went hhhhome to May-hi-co three days ago."

"Doa you know when she'lla be back?"

"Her leetle girl ees bery seek. Señor Cheesling said Consuela will not come back."

I bet he did.

"I am the new hhhhousekeepair. May I hhhhelp you, please?"

Not unless you have commando training.

"Noa thank you."

I hung up the phone. It hit me that everyone who suspected Chisling was behind the Masons' Hall fire had conveniently disappeared.

Everyone, that is, except me.

This was getting scarier all the time.

I suddenly felt like bawling, just bawling my eyes out. It had been almost three days since I'd seen Andy, and it was getting harder and harder to believe I'd ever see her again. Part of me just wanted to call the police.

And I should have.

I know that now.

But I just couldn't.

I was scared for Andy, but I was even scareder for myself. What if my current theory was wrong and

Andy was up to something criminal? She'd left me a message. She could have told me to call the cops. She could have at least hinted. She didn't. Maybe she didn't want anyone finding her.

But what if my theory was right and Chisling had kidnapped her? I knew the answer to that. She was probably dead already. Why would he keep her around?

My mother was a criminal, or my mother was dead. Either way, I'd be put in foster care. I knew a kid that had happened to. He had two nice foster mothers and four rotten ones in three years. I couldn't stand that. I'm only a year younger than Andy was when she started living on the streets. If worst came to worst, I could do it too.

I only sort of believed that. I picked up Andy's keys from the table and looked at them. They were the last connection I had with her. I imagined her opening the door with them. I imagined her scratching her head with them. I imagined them in that old green coat of hers, going shopping with her, going to court with her, heading off to the movies with her...

I was clearly losing it. I was jealous of a set of keys.

I threw them back on the table, and that's when I noticed it. Andy had this ugly pink key chain that you could put a picture in. The picture she'd chosen, of course, was my fifth-grade school photo, the goofy one that caught me right at the height of my Beaver Boy days (honest to God, my teeth were so big I looked like I was chewing on a piano keyboard). Anyway, when I threw down the keys, I noticed that the picture wasn't there.

Then I looked again. The hair on my arms sprang up like toothbrush bristles.

The picture was there. It was just flipped over. Andy had written something on the back.

I'M OK. BIRCHY H. LOVE U. LOVE U. LOVE U.

CHAPTER THIRTY-FIVE

Vi et armis (Latin)
With force and arms

I spent the night getting ready. I tried to think what I needed.

A knife?

A crowbar?

A cat-o'-nine-tails?

Oh, geech. I'd clearly played too many violent video games during my formative years. Like, who did I think I was? A hit man? I wouldn't even make a decent hit boy. I was just some scrawny kid who had to find his mother.

Or what was left of her.

I wasn't going to bother with any of that stuff. I just took the walkie-talkies that came with my old spy kit. I made sure the batteries were okay and then stuffed them in my jacket. I took the $58.72 left in the Player's tobacco tin and put it in my pocket with the last of the Oreos. (I'm a regular commando, eh? Packing a snack for recess. You'd think I'd be embarrassed to admit it.)

As soon as it was open, I stopped at Toulany's for a couple of bottles of pop and then headed off to the Commons. It was Saturday. I knew Kendall would be there early, before the bowl got too crowded. He wasn't a knife or a crowbar, but he could help. Better still, he would help. He was that kind of guy.

I knew I shouldn't have asked him, but I had to. I couldn't do it on my own.

I was too scared. I wanted someone to come with me. I told myself if anything went wrong, if we had to do something we shouldn't, he was still under eighteen and would be tried in youth court. Maybe the judge would go easy on him. That made me feel not quite so bad for asking.

He'd just stepped onto his board and was getting ready to roll into the bowl when I saw him. I yelled, "Hey, Kendall!" I guess I screamed a little louder than I meant to, because he gave me this crazy look and then did something I never thought I'd see Kendall Rankin do.

He fell.

Like, *smash!* Right on this big concrete curb.

I gave him a bottle of pop to put on his swollen eye and some more-or-less clean Kleenex to stop the blood where his tooth had come out. Then I told him all about Andy and Byron and Consuela and Big Bob Chisling. It took me a long time to explain everything, and Kendall kept looking up at me like, *So where's the punch line?* After a while—around the time I got to the part about the Haliburton Building—I could tell he'd stopped expecting me to break into a Daffy Duck impression. He realized I was telling the truth.

When I finished, he just said, "How are we going to get there?" I didn't even have to ask.

He let this kid he barely knew borrow his skateboard for the day, and we went to find a cab.

Kendall probably should have changed his T-shirt or at least wiped the blood off it, because none of the taxi drivers lined up in front of the mall would take us. I even showed them the money. Counted it out for them. Held it up to the light so they could see it was genuine. No one would go for it.

I could sort of understand. A kid who looks about eleven and a six-foot thug impersonator with a black eye and a lip swelled up like an Italian sausage probably aren't your ideal passengers—but still!

It wasn't fair. I had the money. Geez. What else did they want?

I was getting frantic. I tried to talk some sense into this one driver, but he just kept yammering right over me, "I don't care. I ain't gonna take ya. I ain't gonna take ya. I ain't gonna take ya."

That's when I heard someone say, "I'll take you, Cyril. Where would you like to go?"

I turned around and saw Atula coming out of the mall. Could there have been a worse time to run into her?

I was going to lie and say we were going to the movies or something, but Big Mouth Taxi Driver went, "You'll be sorry, lady. They want to go all the jeezly way out to Birchy Head!"

"And so I shall take them!" Atula said, all uppity. She made it very clear that she didn't approve of him not driving us just because of our age and appearance. I was half ready for her to announce that she would forthwith sue him for discrimination under Section Something Something Something of the Canadian Charter of Rights and Freedoms.

The good thing was, Atula made those cab drivers look like jerks. The bad thing was, we were going to spend forty-five minutes in a car with her. She was bound to figure out we were up to something.

I made up some story about us going hiking out there, and I knew right away she was suspicious. (You can always tell by the eyebrows.)

When I introduced Kendall, she was even more suspicious (she had the eyebrows and lips both going). She'd obviously heard Andy talk about him, and I admit, the bashed-up face and bloody T-shirt weren't showing him at his best. But Atula managed to smile anyway and kept up a pretty steady stream of conversation all the way out to St. Margaret's Bay.

She asked a lot of questions about Andy, and I tried to be as vague as I could. "Gee, I haven't seen much of her the last little while." "Oh, you know Andy—always up to no good, ha-ha!" and of course the old "She's been tied up a lot lately." I almost laughed. I like sick puns, and that was about as sick as they get. I mean, how else could Bob hang on to a wolverine like Andy for four days if she wasn't tied up?

Or worse. *Don't think about it. Don't think about it. Don't think about it.*

I guess Atula thought I was uncomfortable talking about Andy (I mean, Atula *had* just fired her), because she eventually changed the subject. She told me all about her clients. At another time I would have been really interested in hearing what everybody was up to. Right then, though, my mind was on other stuff. I just went, "Uh-huh…uh-huh" and "oh yeah?" until I saw a road sign that said *Birchy Head Yacht Club*. I went, "Stop here," a little more suddenly than I should have, I guess, because Atula slammed on the brakes, and we fishtailed on the road for a while.

Atula said, "What?! What?! You want to get out here?!? In the middle of nowhere?!"

I finally managed to convince her that the hiking trail started just on the other side of the yacht club and—I thought I was really brilliant when I came up with this—that Kendall's father was meeting us there. In fact, I said he was going to drive us home, so everything was going to be absolutely A-OK, and she could get back to her shopping, ha-ha!

Atula did this duck thing with her lips, and I knew she wasn't very happy about leaving us out there, but I gave her a kiss and thanked her and bolted out of the car before she could do anything about it. She "but-but-butted" for a while, then finally just gave up and left. Kendall and I stood on the side of the road, waving at her like two little old grannies until she disappeared around the bend.

Kendall looked at me and said, "Now what?"

Good question.

CHAPTER THIRTY-SIX

Trespass II

We ducked past a No Trespassing sign and started to sneak down this winding dirt road to the yacht club. We were in the middle of what looked like a major forest—at least, it did to me, though that's not saying much. I was an underprivileged city kid. The most trees I'd ever seen in one place were on the YMCA's Christmas tree lot.

It was so quiet, you wouldn't believe it—just this crunching sound from us walking on the leaves. I'd heard that's what people like about being out in the country—the peace and tranquility (and, of course, being able to savor a delicious cup of homestyle instant cappuccino). But to tell you the truth, all that nature was creeping me out. I was starting to feel doomed. If Bob Chisling didn't get us, I figured the bears would. And from the look of this place, it would be years before anyone would come by and find the leftovers.

What a way to go.

The only thing that made me feel better was the thought of Mary MacIsaac crying when she heard I'd disappeared. Then I realized she'd probably be crying harder for Kendall, and I started feeling even worse than I had before.

We went around a bend in the road and suddenly the yacht club was right there. You'd swear it actually jumped out at us from the way we both dove into the woods. Some spies, eh? But that was okay. It was good for a laugh, especially when I horked out the big hunk of moss I inhaled when I face-planted.

Kendall had to stop the bleeding from his mouth again, so I started looking around.

I pushed some branches aside and scanned the property. The yacht club was this big old white building with green trim and a wooden verandah that went all the way around the outside. There was also a boathouse right on the water, a boarded-up canteen and a couple of garages at the back of the gravel parking lot. Andy could have been in any one of those buildings. In fact, I half wondered if this wasn't Bob Chisling's Own Private Prison Camp, jam-packed with people who'd caught him doing something he shouldn't.

I'd find out soon enough.

The plan was that I'd scout out the property, and Kendall would stay put and stand guard. It was a pretty good place for a lookout—he was hidden, but he could still see just about everything except the water side of the buildings.

If he heard someone coming down the driveway, he was supposed to warn me on his walkie-talkie. If I found something, I was supposed to call him on mine. He'd either run back to the gas station we'd passed along the way and call for help, or, in the case of a bear attack, try to lure Winnie-the-Killer-Pooh away with the Oreo cookies.

I got out my walkie-talkie and turned it on. I reached in my other pocket for Kendall's walkie-talkie, and I could not believe it.

It wasn't there.

It wasn't in my other pockets.

It wasn't in the woods or on the road. I felt like screaming, though under the circumstances, I realized, that would be a pretty dumb thing to do. Instead I quietly slammed my head against a tree a couple of times.

Kendall got me by the shoulders and said, hey, it wasn't that big a deal. He could still stand guard. If he saw someone coming, he'd just pretend he was lost in the woods and ask them to take him back to the gas station. That would give me a chance to get out of there before they showed up again.

Fine. Good enough.

I waited for a while, and I guess Kendall thought I was scared (gee, where would he get that impression?), because he said that he'd go instead if I liked. I said no, that I wanted to do it. Andy was my mother, after all, and I'd rather take my chances with Bob at the yacht club than with the bears in the woods (I kept that last part to myself).

I snuck out from behind the trees, bolted over to the side of the canteen and pinned my back against the wall. I was shaking and gasping and worried I was going to wet my pants, but I knew Kendall was watching me, so I had to keep going. I crept out and began to look around the canteen. I couldn't see in the windows—they were all boarded up—so I knocked on the door and whispered, "Andy! Andy! Are you there?"

She wasn't, or, at least, she was in no condition to answer.

I did this ridiculous high-speed-tiptoe thing over to the main building. I was trying not to make the gravel crunch, but it didn't work. I did, however, manage to do a reasonably accurate impression of a fairy princess. (I don't know how Kendall kept from cracking up.)

I could see into what must have been the kitchen, but the other windows in the main building were boarded up. The back door was padlocked, but I gave it a rattle anyway. It wasn't going anywhere. I shuffled along the verandah with my back to the wall, just like they do in movies, and edged along to the left side of the building.

I turned and looked back at Kendall. I motioned that I was going to check around the front side of the building. He gave me a thumbs-up. I nodded and disappeared around the corner.

I didn't even have time to scream.

CHAPTER THIRTY-SEVEN

Kidnapping
The unlawful act of capturing and holding a person against his or her will

One hand got me from behind and covered my mouth. The other hand had me by the back of my pants and was lifting me off the ground. That's when I realized what an idiot I was for not bringing some protection. Anything.

A baseball bat.

A laser gun.

A really bad case of armpit fungus.

Even a jock strap would have helped right then. Believe me. The guy was giving me the ultimate power wedgie.

I couldn't get any sound out, but I was kicking and swinging my arms as hard as I could. Lot of good it did me.

Underneath those fancy suits of his, Bob Chisling was still just a big, beefy bartender. I guess he was used to throwing two-hundred-pound drunks out onto the street. A ninety-pound kid must have been like a minor rodent problem to him.

He didn't say anything until he'd dragged me inside the yacht club.

"Listen, Bud, I told you once before: construction sites are dangerous."

I took both of my hands and pulled his index finger down enough to say, "What did you do with my mother?"

"Your mother?" He was obviously surprised for a second. Then he squinted at me like he'd just figured something out. It must have been the reddish hair and freckles. He started dragging me again.

We got to the men's washroom and he put me in a headlock while he rooted in his pockets for the key. I don't know exactly what I was thinking right then, but I can tell you it wasn't good.

He opened the door and threw me in.

I was so worried about slamming headfirst into the urinal that I didn't notice who was there.

Then Andy went, "Listen, you [beep]ing [beep], when are you going to grow up and—" She stopped when she realized it was me sliding across the floor and started screaming and kissing me and crying.

I didn't hear the door lock again, but it must have. Byron was helping us both up, and Consuela was trying to give Andy some toilet paper to wipe her face, but she kept pushing them both away. Normally I would have pushed her away too. I'm a little old for public displays of affection. But right then I didn't care. I was just so glad to see Andy alive and still swearing at people.

We were both trying to get the blubbering under control when the door opened again, and Kendall bounced off a stall and hit the floor. Chisling was in the doorway, pointing a gun at us with one hand and wiping hostage dust off his pants with the other.

"All right!" he said in this kind of crazy-man growl. "What do you want for lunch?"

Gee! Lunch! That was a nice surprise.

Andy got up off the floor, and I could tell right away she wasn't going to offer to help with the sandwiches.

"Better order the Party Pack," she said. "We've got quite a crowd here." She smiled at me and said in her sweetest voice, "Wasn't the big [beep]ing [beep beep] nice to organize this little family reunion for us?"

I said, "Andy…" but there was no way she'd stop. She was like a Doberman in attack mode, and none of us was brave enough to try strapping a muzzle on her. She turned on Chisling again.

"Oh, you're a regular [*beep*]ing he-man, aren't you? Not only did you manage to overpower a runty, undernourished cleaning lady, a two-pack-a-day smoker and a one-armed beanpole—you also managed to bag two infants! Wow! Really impressive! I mean, look at this fine specimen you dragged in!"

I couldn't believe it. My own mother was publicly mocking my physique. She yanked up my T-shirt and ran her fingers up and down my ribs like she was playing some primitive bony instrument. She put on this phony Southern accent and went, "Oh, you big strong man, you! How'd you evah rassle this ferocious beast to the ground? I git shivers just a-thinkin' 'bout it!"

Chisling's left eyelid twitched, and I could tell he was getting agitated. I pulled my T-shirt down and whispered, "Quit it, Andy!"

Andy glared at me as if I was on Chisling's side. I should have known better. Like she was going to listen to reason? This was just the excuse she needed to take off on a major rant.

"No, don't you tell me to quit it! I mean it! I'm tired of this guy lording it over us. We're all pretending he's some big [*beep*]ing deal just because he's got a gun. Well, [*beep*] that. He's a wuss. He's pathetic, trying to bribe us with burgers! To get us to pretend that none of this happened! Oh yeah, Bob, just a few more days together, and I'm sure we'll come up with a set of facts that we can all agree on. Ha [*beep*]ing ha!"

She was practically nose to nose with Chisling now, and I could tell he wasn't keen on her breath. "Well, I'd love to be able to say that we all just decided to take a week-long holiday in the charming men's room of the Birchy Head Yacht Club—but that's not what happened, now is it, Mis-ter Chis-ling? You killed a man for a parking space. You [*beep*]ing bullied Consuela into burning down that building for you. Then, when you found out we knew what you were up to, you: (a) tricked me into coming here; (b) kidnapped Consuela; and (c) practically bashed the [*beep*]ing brains out of Byron, threw him in the trunk of your car and dumped him out here too. That's our 'mutually agreed-upon set of facts,' and a thousand Big [*beep*]ing Macs aren't going to change a word of it, right, guys?"

Everyone nodded.

"And if you don't like it, you may as well just blow our brains out right now! C'mon, Bob. Be a man! You got a gun. Use it!"

Everyone stopped nodding and started going, "Andy! AN-DY!!!" Was she nuts? Suddenly we were all in this complete panic. If I'd had a sock handy, I would have stuffed it in that big mouth of hers.

She was screaming, Byron was trying to grab her, Consuela was going, "Please? Please?" because she didn't know what was happening, and Chisling was waving the gun at us. The cubicle walls were rattling, and the sounds were bouncing off the ceiling, and I knew it wouldn't be long before something terrible happened.

I was right.

Chisling grabbed me by the neck and held the gun to my head.

That did it.

That shut everybody up. (Kendall kept his hand over Andy's mouth, just to be on the safe side. Or maybe just to keep her upright. She'd gone pretty pale all of a sudden.)

Chisling said, "Okay. I said, what…do you want… for lunch? Consuela? *¿Qué quieres para el almuerzo?*"

"Taco Bell, *por favor*, Señor."

"*Está bien*. Byron?"

"Large Greek salad, extra olives and a green tea."

"Andy?"

Kendall moved his hand down just enough for her to answer.

"A large bacon cheeseburger and fries."

"Kid with the bloody face?"

"Ah, same as her, I guess."

"You?"

Having a gun to my head kind of killed my appetite.

"Nothing."

Andy pried off Kendall's hand and went, "You're eating something."

I went, "I'm not hungry."

She went, "You're eating something. Look how skinny you are."

I said, "Would you leave me alone! I'm not hungry."

Then Chisling got into it. "Do as your mother says. You're having something to eat."

This was nuts. One of them's got a gun to my head, the other one's saying, "C'mon, blow our brains out!" but they're both concerned about me meeting my daily nutritional requirements. Like that makes sense. Adults. At what point in the aging process is it, exactly, that the brain turns to mush?

"Okay. Okay," I said. "I'll have a cheeseburger too."

That seemed to make him happy. He threw me to the floor and left.

Andy screamed out after him, "And get me a supersized Coke too, you [*beep*]ing [*beep beep*]." She started banging on the door. "Did you hear me? Did you hear me, YOU [*BEEP*]ING WUSS? I WANT A COKE!!!"

I heard Chisling make this grunting sound, and then these big crashing footsteps started coming toward us, and I thought, Oh no. That's it. Andy has finally done it. He's going to kill us all.

Two seconds later the door to the washroom flew open again, and Atula fell in.

CHAPTER THIRTY-EIGHT

False imprisonment
The confinement of a person without just cause

Atula ordered a chicken sub (extra mayo, tomatoes, hot peppers), and Chisling left again. After the introductions and the kisses and hugs and apologies, we all started trying to figure out how everyone had ended up in the men's room of a boarded-up yacht club.

We had quite a bit of time to put the pieces together. Andy said it always took Chisling at least an hour and a half to pick up the food. He didn't want anyone getting suspicious, so he'd drive right back into town and pick up each person's meal at a different place. The guy had everything worked out, except what he was going to do with us.

Anyway, back to how we all got there.

You know about Kendall and me, so I'm not going to go into that again. It was a little more complicated for everybody else.

CHAPTER THIRTY-NINE

Confession

An admission of guilt

ATULA

"I blame myself. I am entirely to blame. I am very ashamed to admit it, but it's true. When Mr. Chisling called that day and said you had not shown up for his meeting, I accepted it as another example of your increasingly irresponsible behavior, Andy. I did not even consider the possibility that something might have happened to you. I was so angry, I did not even bother to telephone and ask you for an explanation. I only thought of how your missing an appointment with 'our friend' would negatively impact on the social standing of my law firm. Had I had the least bit of faith in you, I would have tried to reach you, I would have realized you were gone, I would have called the police—and Mr. Chisling would in all likelihood be behind bars today!...

"No, no, Andy. Don't be so quick to forgive me. My behavior was even worse than that. I fired you without even the decency to tell you myself, and then...and then this thing with the boys. They wouldn't be here if it were not for my ridiculous ego...

"I am sorry, but you are wrong, Cyril. I did not drive you here as a favor. I drove you here—again my apologies, Andy—because I no longer trusted your mother. I did not consider her lifelong devotion to you. I thought only of her few short weeks of erratic work habits and concluded that she was an inadequate parent. I took great pleasure, I assure you, in offering to solve your problem with the taxi drivers and take you myself. I thought, What a marvelous person I am compared to that wretched Andy, who is no doubt sitting in front of the television set, smoking cigarettes all day, instead of looking after her only child...

"I am very lucky you can laugh at these things, Andy, especially given our situation, but no, I do not have a cigarette I could give you now. In fact, the one good thing Mr. Chisling may have managed to do is force you to quit that disgusting habit...

"Now, now! Enough of that language, Andy! You're causing me to forget where I was. Oh yes.

I picked up the boys at the mall, and after my initial thrill at being their knight in shining armor, I began to feel suspicious. What, I asked myself, was Cyril doing with such a large amount of cash? (He certainly did not earn it working at Varma and Associates.) Why did he so desperately need to go to Birchy Head? And who was this dangerous-looking character he had chosen to travel with? Again, I apologize. Kendall, you really are the most lovely young man, and I had no right to jump to such conclusions, regardless of how many teeth you may or may not have.

"I was not able to come up with a plausible reason why I should accompany the boys on their hike, so felt I had no choice but to leave them alone in the wilds of Birchy Head. I set off back to town in a state of some agitation. Those boys were up to no good, I was sure of it. I considered hiding in the woods and 'tailing' them, as they say on American television, but I could not in good conscience do so. Too many of my clients' lives are made miserable by unfounded suspicion. They are always the first to be blamed simply because they are too poor, too black, too old or, for that matter, too young.

"Then I saw your walkie-talkie, Cyril, lying on the floor of my car, and I thought to myself, Aha!

That's the ticket. I was, of course, just as suspicious as before, but at least now I had a reason to go back—I needed to return your equipment. I 'hung a U-ey' and flew back to Birchy Head.

"I had no idea where you might have got to by this time, so I parked my car where I had let you off and headed down the Yacht Club drive. It was rather unnerving. I felt afraid, walking alone on a deserted laneway, and I clutched my only weapon— your walkie-talkie. In doing so, I accidentally turned it on. As you can imagine, I was quite surprised— but not alarmed—to hear Mr. Chisling's voice. I had heard he owned the yacht club and thought he was just being the perfect host by taking lunch orders. I beg your pardon, Cyril?…Well, I guess you must have forgotten to turn yours off, because I certainly heard you speaking.

"At first, as you can imagine, I was hugely relieved. Against all odds, I'd found you! I ran down to the yacht club, saw Mr. Chisling's lovely green car parked in front and raced in. By the time I heard Andy demanding her '[beep]ing Coke,' it was too late. Mr. Chisling had me by the scarf and was rather brutally frog-marching me into the men's room."

CHAPTER FORTY

CONSUELA (TRANSLATED BY BYRON)

"Señor Bob said I stole ten thousand dollars, but I didn't steal ten thousand dollars. I didn't steal ten cents. He said he had proof and that I would get deported or go to jail and never see my children again.

"I didn't know what to do. I didn't want to tell anybody. I was so ashamed and scared. I overheard a Guatemalan man at the Immigration Resource Center. He was talking about his lawyer, Atula. He said she helps all immigrants. On my day off I went to Atula's office. I was going to tell her everything. I hoped she would solve my problem. I waited all day in her office, and it was almost time for her to see me, but then she said something to Andy's son. I heard her say Señor Chisling's name. I was so afraid, I ran away immediately and never came back.

"Again, I didn't know what to do. No one could help me. Señor Bob is an important man. All the people here love him. All the immigrants here love him because he looks after them. He does nice things. Nobody here loves me. Nobody would believe me if I said I didn't steal the money. Nobody would believe me if I said this nice man wanted me to burn down a building.

"I was very afraid. I said I would do it. It was just a dirty old building. Nobody would get hurt. Señor Bob left some equipment for making drugs in the Haliburton Building next door. I snuck in at six in the evening, when everybody had gone. At midnight I climbed in the back window of the Masons' Hall, just like Señor Bob told me to do. I set up the equipment against a wall. I put newspapers around it. I poured on gasoline. I lit the match, and I ran, very afraid. I looked back only once. That's when I saw the face of Carlos in the upstairs window. He just looked at me.

"I'm sorry. I'm sorry! I am very, very sorry! I tried to save him. I tried. But I am too small, and the fire was too big."

CHAPTER FORTY-ONE

Confession III

BYRON

"Karl was a buddy of mine from the old days. He wasn't so bad then. The schizophrenia got a lot worse later. But what can you do? You can't force a person to take their pills unless you can prove they're going to hurt somebody. The law won't let you. Most of the time, Karl wouldn't have dreamed of hurting nobody. He was a pretty gentle guy. But when them voices in his head started yelling at him, you didn't know what he was going to do.

"Anyway, that night I checked all his old stomping grounds but couldn't find him anywhere. I was getting some worried. He'd been acting pretty strange lately, and I figured he was off his meds again.

"Just after midnight, I decided to try the Masons' Hall, see if he'd camped out there. I come around the corner on Barrington Street and I got a whiff of smoke, and I thought, Oh my jeez, what's Karl gone and done now? I kicked in a window 'round back and crawled in.

"That's when I saw Consuela. She was screaming in Spanish that there was a man upstairs. Her arm was all burned to bejazus and she was crying and trying to get up the stairs, but the smoke was so thick by this time you could hardly see your hand in front of you. I called up to Karl, and I'm not sure if he answered or not, because right about then the ceiling started falling in. I pretty much had to drag Consuela, but I got her out about two seconds before the whole thing come down.

"Her arm was a mess, and mine wasn't too good either, but neither of us wanted to go to the hospital. My shirt was pretty clean, so I took out my Swiss Army knife and tore it up into bandages and fixed us up as good as I could. I guess I must have left the knife on the ground when I heard the sirens starting up. I figure that's where they got my fingerprints. Anyways, I dragged Consuela out through the back alleys to Spring Garden Road.

"She was hysterical. She kept screaming about her babies and Karl and some *señor* she knew. I didn't understand everything she was saying. All I got was that someone had forced her into this. I promised I'd help her. I got her phone number and told her to run like hell.

"I hid out for a few days. I didn't know what to do. People knew I was going to look for Karl at the Masons' Hall that night. I figured they were my friends, but you never know. One of them might have fingered me for burning the place down. I couldn't take the chance of getting seen again. I wasn't ready to go back to Dorchester Pen. I done my time.

"Part of me just wanted to take off, but I'd promised Consuela I'd help her. How? I didn't know. All I knew was, she needed legal help, and I hated lawyers. Scum of the earth, far as I was concerned. My opinion had been pretty much confirmed a coupla weeks before all this crap happened when I realized that the lady lawyer at the Poverty Coalition rally was Squeaky. At the time, I was glad she hadn't seen me. Like I say, lawyers in general are scum of the earth, and Squeaky was one in particular I didn't care to encounter.

"But then the fire happened. What could I do? I looked Squeaky up. Time I called in some favors, I figured.

"That's not what Andy figured though. She didn't want me around. She didn't want to hear about Consuela. And she really didn't want me saying nothing inflammatory about Bob Chisling, her new idol…

"He was so, Andy. That's exactly how you thought of him…Did too!…You did. Admit it!…

"Okay, sorry, you're right, Cyril. No use arguing about that now—'specially since I'm right. Nyuk, nyuk, nyuk.

"Anyway, for *whatever* reason, your mother was not open to helping me, so I had to play hardball. It took me about a month, but I finally got her to talk to Consuela. Our little meeting went okay— Andy was at least willing to look into things—so I figured I'd done my part. I took Consuela to lunch, she went to pick up the Chisling kids after school, and I headed out to Seaview Park for a hike. It felt some good. First bit of freedom I'd had in a month. At about five, five thirty, I went back to the apartment and was just packing my bags to go when there was a knock at the door, and my lights went out. Still don't know what the big ape hit me with."

CHAPTER FORTY-TWO

Confession IV

ANDY

"See, Cyril? This is why I'm always after you to watch what you're doing. You screw up once as a kid, and you'll spend the rest of your life paying for it...

"No, I don't mean I screwed up by having you, and you know it! I mean I screwed up when I, ah, had that little...you know...incident in the, ah, church. Anyway! Enough about that. You wanted to know how I got to the yacht club...

"Byron tracked me down, like he said, and, yeah, okay, I admit it. I wasn't immediately convinced that Chisling had done anything wrong. It didn't take me long to come around, though...

"It didn't!...

"Excuse me...

"Excuse me!...Would you SHUT UP PLEASE?...

"I'm starting to get annoyed here…

"Okay. If you want to hear my side of the story, Byron's got to shut.

"His.

"[Beep]ing.

"Yap.

"I mean it. I don't know what he thinks is so funny. I came around! I'm here, aren't I?…

"Oh, for [beep]'s sake, SHUT UP!

"Okay. Thank you, Mr. Cuvelier. Where was I? Oh yeah. The part where you threaten me. You guys know about that? Saint Byron the Blackmailer here threatened to ruin my life. Yup. It's true. Guess what, people? He's not perfect!

"Anyway, he threatened me, so I rather sensibly agreed to meet Consuela in the park. I listened to her story, and she sounded sincere, but—apparently because I'm not the incredible judge of character Byron is—I still had my doubts. I mean, Consuela could have been sincere but crazy. Don't bother translating that, okay, Byron? At that point, I couldn't believe Chisling would ever willfully hurt an immigrant. He spent so much time trying to help them! In fact, I was so sure Chisling couldn't be guilty, I decided to do a title search, just to prove it.

"When I saw that estoppel on the Masons' Hall, though, I knew right away that Consuela was telling the truth. You wouldn't believe how pissed off I was! I'd finally met a rich guy with a social conscience, and he turned out to be a worse [*beep beep*] than any of the [*beep*]ing dorks I went to law school with! I wanted to kill the guy right then and there. Strangle him with one of his own two-hundred-dollar ties. Which, come to think of it, isn't such a bad idea…

"Relax! I'm only joking.

"Sort of…

"Anyway, I was supposed to get together with Chisling that day for our regular Immigration Resource Center meeting. I wasn't going to say anything to him about the fire. I was going to get my case all ready and let the cops explain it all to him later, preferably while they were handcuffing him. In the meantime, I was going to go to the meeting and pretend that everything was the same as usual.

"I went home first and put the file in the freezer. Call me paranoid, but I didn't trust Chisling at all by this time. I wouldn't have put it past him to go rifling through my apartment just to check me out. I figured he was too stupid to look in the freezer.

"I took a couple of deep breaths, told myself to stay calm and headed off to our meeting.

Chisling picked me up outside this little coffee place on Argyle Street. He was his usual charming self. *Andy, I love your perfume. You're like a breath of fresh air. Hey, great coat!* You know, the usual disgusting crap. I just smiled and let him do all the talking while we drove to the Immigration Resource Center.

"Everything was fine until he asked me to grab the plans for the new family-health room we're talking about putting in. I leaned over to get them out of the backseat of the car, and that's when I saw it. There was another blueprint there too. For a parking lot! A parking lot where the Masons' Hall used to be.

"Okay, I know it. I'm an idiot. But I couldn't help it! I just lost it. Chisling was acting like he was a big do-gooder, so concerned about the plight of the lowly immigrant. Meanwhile he's basically paving over Karl's grave for a parking lot. What a hypocrite!

"I said, *How can you [beep]ing live with yourself? You think I don't know what you did? There are witnesses!*…

"I know, I know, Cyril! I was a jerk. I should have just shut up like I planned to. But I didn't. Chisling was going, *What do you mean?* and *I have no idea what you're talking about*, and sounding sooo innocent.

"Too innocent. That's when I got kind of freaked out. Worried that I'd never see my little Cy-cy again. I started trying to take back what I said. Pretending I didn't mean it. I started saying that I was sorry, that I must have misunderstood. I said it was probably just a rumor and I was so overworked lately I obviously wasn't thinking clearly.

"Chisling smiled and patted me on the leg and said he understood. He was really overworked too! Suddenly he had this great idea. Why didn't we forget about the Immigration Resource Center just for that day and take a drive? He said he owned a property in the country somewhere and it was really beautiful out there. He claimed it would do me a world of good.

"Ha!

"I didn't want to upset him, so I played along. I said sure, but did he mind if I used his cell phone? I wanted to let my son know I might be back a little late. I thought Chisling would be easy on me if he knew I had a kid. Maybe he would have been, if he'd believed me. But apparently I'm too young to have a thirteen-year-old. That's what he told me yesterday. He thought I was just making it up so he'd go easy on me. Great minds think alike, eh?

"So, anyway, I called you on his phone and left that drippy message. I figured the whole honey-sweetie-mama stuff would make you suspect something, but Chisling wouldn't. I was just about to tell you that you could reach me at his number when he grabbed it from me and hung up.

"*Battery running low*, he said. *Don't want to run out of juice.*

"I tried to stay calm. I figured you'd get the message, realize something was wrong and call Atula when I didn't show up. She'd know what to do with that file. She'd understand Chisling was implicated. I mean, I never expected you to try and solve this yourself, ya dumb cluck!...

"I am so allowed to kiss you.

"I can kiss you as much as I want. See?...

"Okay, okay, Cyril. Geez. If you didn't want me to drool all over you, you shouldn't have tried so hard to find me.

"Anyway, we got about two minutes out of town, and the gas-tank thing started going *bing, bing*. Chisling was on empty, but he wouldn't stop. I guess he didn't want some gas jockey seeing me in his car and blabbing to the police when I went missing.

"So Chisling kept going, and the gas-tank thing kept *bing*ing, so about twenty clicks down the road he finally gave in and pulled up at a self-serve. He's the type of guy who never sweats—worried it'll ruin one of his nice shirts, I guess—but he was sweating then. That's what was scaring me the most. Those little drops hanging off his eyebrows.

"I should have just run for it right then, but I didn't. Don't know why. I was scared, I guess. Or worried that if it turned out Consuela was lying, I'd look like a [*beep*]ing idiot. Anyway, I didn't. Best I could do was just scribble that note to you on my key chain and drop it out the window while Chisling was filling the tank. I never really believed it would make it back to you in time. I just wanted you to know if anything happened to me that I love you, even when you make that I'm-going-to-barf face.

"Anyway, Chisling was still pretending we were just on a nice little country drive. He took me on a lovely tour of the Birchy Head Yacht Club that ended, somewhat unceremoniously, when he booted me into the men's room and locked the door. A few hours later Consuela and Byron got the tour too. It took us a couple of days to calm Consuela down. She was so upset about telling on Byron. But it wasn't her fault. Chisling had her terrified.

"I was really scared at first too. But then when Chisling didn't kill us the first day, I figured he wasn't going to. I just told myself, *You got to have faith.* Cyril will tell Atula, Atula will tell the cops, and the cops will catch Chisling. I figured I could hold out until then. No way was I going to let Chisling think, even for a minute, that he'd beat me.

"You know, I lost all respect for that man. I mean, *all* respect. I don't respect him as a human being. I don't even respect him as a kidnapper. The guy's such a loser. You know, eventually he's going to let us go, but only because he's too chicken to do anything else. What a [*beep*]ing wuss."

CHAPTER FORTY-THREE

Bribery and corruption
Giving or offering any reward to any person to influence his or her conduct

"So what are we going to do about it then?" I said.

"Do about what?" Andy went.

She drives me crazy sometimes.

"The skyrocketing cost of toenail clippers!" I rolled my eyes. "Geez, Andy, a homicidal maniac has us locked up. What do you think I'm talking about?"

Atula jumped in. "Cyril, your sarcasm is completely uncalled for." Andy stuck her tongue out at me like she was in second grade or something. "However, I do think you raise a valid question." I stuck my tongue out at Andy and pumped my fist in the air. "What *are* we going to do?"

Byron answered. "Here's our options as I see 'em. One, walk out the door. We tried that. It's locked, and Andy's tweezers didn't do no good prying it open.

"Two, crawl out the window. Tried that too. It's locked, and it's boarded up from the outside.

"Three, scream at the top of our lungs and hope some moose hunter hears us. Tried that too. It just gave me a sore throat, though Andy seemed to enjoy it.

"Four, we all gang up and jump Chisling. We didn't try that. He's got a gun, and we don't. So there you have them. Our options."

I was, like, wild. "Oh, c'mon! There are other things we can do!"

"Yeah? Like what?" Byron said.

"Well…" I was thinking as hard as I could. "Kick down the door!"

"Oh, sorry. Tried that one too. What do you think those dents are from?"

"Okay, okay! Well, what about…the drains! Couldn't we pull the toilets off and crawl out that way?"

Andy said, "After you, Cyril!" and started laughing like some old drunk. I mean, I didn't relish dog paddling through…let's just say *human waste* either, but I thought we should at least consider it.

Byron said, "Even if you could hold your breath that long, the sewage pipe ain't wide enough. Didn't you never see a sewage pipe?"

I was just about to lay into everybody for being so negative when Kendall leaned over and whispered, "Byron's right."

Instead I just went, "Okay, then. So what are we going to do? Just sit here until Chisling breaks down and admits he made a terrible mistake?"

All I wanted was an answer.

I got a demonstration.

Byron jumped up and said, "Exactly—except we ain't going to sit."

Me and my big mouth had just reminded him that it was time, if you can believe this, for our "aerobics class."

As if I hadn't had enough exercise that day.

As if it was a good idea to make six people trapped in a tiny bathroom work up a sweat.

As if the place didn't stink bad enough as it was.

I figured Andy wasn't going to go for aerobics class either. Her idea of exercise was stretching across the table for an ashtray. But suddenly she was Buffy Buffbody. She grabbed me by the arm and went, "Get up, Cyril! Quit groaning! Byron's right. He's the one who's done time. He knows how to survive a prison situation. If we all want to keep our sanity until Chisling gives in, we've got to stick to a routine, look after our health, keep our minds and bodies strong!"

Once again an alien had taken over my mother's body, but this one looked mean. I wasn't going to take any chances. I got up and did Byron's stupid stretching routine.

The only thing that made it bearable at all was that I got to "accidentally" kick Andy in the bum every time I did a leg curl. It felt good, but not good enough to make me forget what was about to happen. No matter how hard I pumped or lunged, I just couldn't quit thinking that Chisling was coming back to off us. I could picture him outside right that very moment, pouring gasoline around the yacht club and lighting the match.

Could you blame him? What choice did he have? Andy had made it clear she wasn't going to be bribed or blackmailed into keeping her mouth shut. And if he got rid of Andy, he was going to have to get rid of all of us. And he'd better do it fast before anyone noticed we were gone. At least, that's what I'd be thinking if I were him.

I heard the sound of a car pulling into the driveway, and my whole body went *doink*. A lot of good all that stretching had done. It's hard to stay loose when you hear the guy with the gun show up. Andy heard the car too, but she just smiled and said, "Lunch!" She was acting like the school bell had just rung and there were Dunkaroos for dessert. Byron made us all wash our hands. (Can you believe this guy?)

I was waiting for my turn at the air blower when Andy nudged me and said, "Aren't you glad I made you order something?" I smiled, though it wasn't what you'd call a real cheery smile. By that time I figured, Well, it's over. At least we're together. Better than being mauled in the woods by a bear, or Andy dying out here all alone and me never knowing what happened to her.

I looked around the room. Kendall was sitting on the floor, studying his nails like he'd never seen fingers before—or maybe like he'd never see them again. Under the circumstances, that was more likely, I guess. I felt really bad about dragging him into this. He'd had nothing to do with any of it. He was just being a good guy, as usual, helping me out. You can see where that gets you.

And Atula. It was my stupid fault she was there too. I should have just lied, come up with some dumb reason why she couldn't take us out to Birchy Head. I could have said I was carsick or had left the stove on or forgot I had an appointment at the Adolescent Growth Clinic. I could have said anything.

I should have said anything.

If Andy and I died together, big deal. The world would go on. We just had us. Who else cared? But if something happened to Kendall or Atula, tons of people would be really sad. Kendall had his little sister and his dad and his mother, who wasn't doing too good since his dad left, and, of course, Mary MacIsaac. Atula had her son and her parents and Toby and Marge and Mr. Lucas and Elmore Himmelman and even Darlene and Freddie. People needed her. Consuela had her kids at home in Mexico. I don't know who Byron had, but it didn't matter. He'd already done enough for us.

This really sucked. It sucked more than anything in my life had ever sucked.

"Is there something in your eye?" Andy said, and I said, "Nah, it's just the toilet disinfectant getting to me, I guess."

The washroom door opened, and Chisling pushed a box in with his foot. He kept the gun aimed at us.

"There you go. They didn't have any green tea, so I had to get Byron Red Zinger."

Andy grabbed the box and started handing out the food.

"It's [beep]ing cold!" she said. "What were you doing out there? Going for a Sunday drive?" She gave him this what-a-jerk face and went back to tossing people their lunches.

She opened the last brown paper bag to see whose it was. All I could see was the back of her head, but I knew right away that something was wrong.

"What the [beep] is this?" My first thought was that Big Bob must have slipped her a nice juicy dead-rat-burger for lunch.

Andy jumped up and started waving the package in Chisling's face. She was wild.

"I said, what the [beep] is this supposed to be?"

Chisling tried to look cool.

"It's my last offer, Andy, that's what it is. A hundred thousand dollars. Take it or leave it. It's your choice."

One hundred thousand dollars.

One hundred thousand dollar bills.

One thousand hundred dollar bills.

It was such a pleasant thought.

So comforting.

Bob would put the gun away and give us each a big pile of money and we could all go home. I felt light. Like I didn't weigh anything at all. Like any second I might start floating around the men's wash-room, like an astronaut in a space module.

A rich astronaut.

An astronaut with a new skateboard and brand-name clothing waiting for him at home on planet Earth.

Andy shot that spaceship down pretty fast.

"That's what we've been trying to tell you all along, Bob. There is no [beep]ing choice here. You killed a man, and nothing you can do will ever make us forget it."

Andy biffed the wad of money at Chisling. Most of it got him in the head, but a few bills broke away from the pack and sort of fluttered around for a few seconds like little hundred-dollar ballerinas.

Chisling whacked one out of the way and looked at Andy like he was going to kill her.

Andy looked right back at him.

I suppose I should have been proud. You know, my mother standing up for what's right and all that. But to tell you the truth, I was really just hoping that someone would pipe up and say, "Whoa, whoa. Now wait a minute here, Andy. Maybe Mr. Chisling has a point."

I looked around the room. Byron had already gone to jail for helping someone. Atula's whole life was about sticking up for people who couldn't stick up for themselves. Consuela had seen Karl die, and I knew she'd do anything to make up for it. I ruled them out.

I was sort of hopeful about Kendall. Maybe he'd say something. But he was standing beside Byron now, with his head up and his shoulders back, looking at Andy like she was Nelson Mandela. I knew he was on their side.

That left me. But if I said anything, Andy would kill me. Better Chisling killed me—then I'd at least go out like a hero. I actually thought exactly that, but it still wasn't my first choice. Die a chicken or die a hero? Frankly, neither appealed to me.

I wanted to live.

I wanted to skateboard.

I wanted to at least kiss a girl.

I wanted to see the new Jackie Chan movie.

I wanted to live long enough to hit five foot nine.

Even five six, five four, five three. I didn't care.

I just wanted to live.

Chisling went, "ALL RIGHT!" and I thought he was going to line us up against the wall right then and blow us away. "I'll throw in a nice three-bedroom condo at Haliburton Place, but that's my final offer. I mean it."

Andy took two steps toward him and went, "[*Beep*]. Off."

Chisling's face turned purple. His fingers started toying with the gun. He moved his neck back and forth like his collar had suddenly gotten too tight.

I believe this is what they refer to as an "explosive situation."

For a second there, all I could think was, Why didn't Andy ever take me to church? It would have been handy to know a prayer right about then.

But I didn't know a prayer or even who I'd say it to. So I had to come up with something else.

I said, "Mr. Chisling?"

He turned and looked at me. "What?"

I said, "My hands are greasy. I can't open this package of ketchup."

I held it out like I wanted him to help me. He stepped forward. He was a dad, after all. I guess helping kids with ketchup is sort of an instinct. As soon as he got within firing range, I squeezed the little tinfoil package as hard as I could. Ketchup splatted all over that nice gray suit of his.

You'd swear I'd barfed on him. He jumped back and went, "Aii! Ffff! My Prada jacket!" He looked down at the mess, and that's when I lunged at him. I dug my Beaver Boy fangs into his hand, and the gun went flying. Andy scrambled after it. Chisling went to grab her, but Consuela's extra-hot taco got him dead in the eye. Kendall did this kickflip thing I've seen him do on his skateboard. Chisling went down like a bowling pin, and we all winced when his head hit the knee Byron had waiting for him.

We stood there for a couple of seconds, admiring his big conked-out carcass, and then panic kicked in. I guess we'd all seen too many movies where the guy you think is dead suddenly jerks back to life and starts hacking at people.

Chisling didn't. He just lay there with his tongue in his ear. It didn't matter. Everybody started screaming, "Quick! Quick!" and "Go! Go! Go!" I grabbed Chisling's keys out of his pocket, and Kendall tied his arms up with Atula's scarf. We were just locking the bathroom door behind us when we heard him start to moan.

We took off. We didn't even take the money. We ran with our bellies out and our arms pumping. Even Consuela looked like she was going for a medal.

We all piled into Bob's big green BMW, and Andy drove us back to the Halifax police station at about 130 clicks an hour.

I've never seen her so happy in my life.

CHAPTER FORTY-FOUR

Arraignment
The act of charging a person with a crime

Blackmail.

Arson.

Murder.

Kidnapping.

Assault and battery.

Forcible confinement.

Unauthorized use of a firearm.

Bribery.

Chisling had the book thrown at him. Considering that five of us had caught him red-handed on the last four charges, you'd think that would be it, wouldn't you? I mean, what more do you need to prove the guy's guilty?

Yeah, but it's not that simple.

The "Masons' Hall affair" was all over the papers, and for a while there it looked like convicting Bob was going to be a slam dunk. But then Chisling got himself some high-priced lawyer from Toronto, and now I don't know anymore.

It will be years before this thing goes to trial. That'll give him plenty of time to come up with some killer defense. His lawyer keeps showing up on the news saying stuff like, "Mr. Chisling is very anxious for this matter to reach the courts. Once the real facts of the case can be heard, we are very confident he will be thoroughly vindicated. He looks forward to being able to put this nightmare behind him so that he can devote himself wholly to the things that matter most to him—his loving family and his service to the community."

I just about gag every time I hear that. What's his case?

That we were all trespassing on his property?

That it was self-defense?

Temporary insanity?

Mistaken identity?

He was sleepwalking when it happened?

I'm not kidding. They've all been tried before. You wouldn't believe the boneheaded defenses people try to get away with. There was this one guy in the States who actually claimed he ate so many Twinkies that he went psycho. He tried to convince the jury it wasn't his fault he killed a man. It was the Twinkies' fault.

No lie. "The Twinkie defense." Look it up on the Internet.

I can just imagine what Big Bob's lawyer is cooking up for him. Pinning the fire on Byron the ex-con? Hey! They found his fingerprint-covered Swiss Army knife on the property, and there are witnesses who'll swear they saw him going to the Masons' Hall that night. It could work.

Blaming Consuela? Who knows? Maybe Chisling will try to turn things around. Say it was actually Consuela who was trying to blackmail him by pretending that he set the fire.

Or it could be that Big Bob will just throw himself on the mercy of the court. The lawyer will be all apologetic and say Mr. Chisling was under a lot of financial stress. He'll admit he went a little crazy, but who wouldn't under the circumstances, what with all those employees to look after and three kids and a wife at home and a heavy, heavy load of volunteer responsibilities! The lawyer will say Chisling never meant to kill anyone—he just wanted to get rid of a building. A building that had sat empty for three years, and if it weren't for some silly laws protecting heritage properties, a building that would have been torn down ages ago. It was an eyesore, he'll say, and he'll wave a bunch of letters from citizens thanking his client for getting rid of that awful old pile of bricks.

And sure, Mr. Chisling took five prisoners, but hey, give the guy some credit! He did feed them well. (He even has the receipts to prove it.)

I don't know. Get the right lawyer, and Bob Chisling could get off. Crazier things have happened.

I guess we'll just have to wait and see.

Until then, life is good. We're big heroes around here. Some film company even gave Andy major dollars to make a movie of her life. Bob Chisling wouldn't call it a fortune, but it was enough for Andy to buy an old car for herself, a new skateboard for me and a front tooth for Kendall.

She and Atula are back working together at— get this—Varma, MacIntyre and Associates. They're spending a lot of time trying to keep Consuela from being deported for setting the fire. It's pretty stressful, but that's okay. They're lawyers. They're not having fun unless they're stressed out.

Byron has a real paying job at the shelter and a real girlfriend too. The weird thing is that after all we've been through, I'm not sure if I'm too happy about the other woman. Andy and he made a pretty good pair, in a twisted sort of way. At least he got her to exercise. I wouldn't even be all that upset anymore if I found out that he was my father. But he's not. That C.C. tattoo on his arm is for his own dad, Clyde Cuvelier. Oh well, at least I don't have to worry about inheriting that weaselly beard of his.

Kendall is still Kendall. He keeps acting like he didn't do anything to bag Chisling. Like he just went along for the ride. Like anyone would have done it. He sort of shrugs it all off, the same way he sort of shrugs off the fact that there's this army of hot girls following his every move. "Oh, them? They're always here. They just like watching kids skateboard." Yeah right. Then how come they aren't watching that kid with the overactive saliva glands doing his stuff?

Someone saw Kendall on TV when the story first broke, and even though he had a black eye, a fat lip and no front tooth, they offered him a spot on these skateboard commercials. He shrugged that off too, but his mother made him take it. I guess they need the money.

And me? I'm back at school. I'm skateboarding. And I'm loving the way Mary MacIsaac suddenly remembers my name.

AUTHOR'S NOTE

My brothers and sister all grew up to be lawyers. I married a lawyer. I watch *Law & Order* whenever I can and am in regular contact with the Halifax Police Department through its very efficient Parking Ticket Enforcement program.

But that's as close as I come to having legal credentials.

I'm sort of like Cyril that way. I've spent a lot of time observing the legal world from the sidelines. It's often fascinating. It's often unbelievably boring (worse, as Cyril noted, than math class). One way or another, though, I've been around lawyers long enough—I hope—to have a rough idea of how things work.

I've been exposed to the Canadian system and have therefore set my story in Nova Scotia. My understanding, though, is that the laws and legal principles described in this book are the same in most countries of the English-speaking world.

At least, I think they are.

But maybe you should check with your lawyer.